Agatha Christie

Why Didn't They Ask Evans?

Collins

Collins

HarperCollins Publishers
77-85 Fulham Palace Road
Hammersmith, London W6 8JB
www.collinselt.com

This *Collins English Readers Edition* published 2012

Reprint 10 9 8 7 6 5 4 3 2 1 0

Original text first published in Great Britain by Collins 1934

ISBN: 978-85-7827-514-3

A catalogue record for this book is available from the British Library.

Educational Consultant: Fitch O'Connell

Cover by crushed.co.uk © HarperCollins/Agatha Christie Ltd 2008

Typeset by Aptara in India

Printed and bound in Great Britain by Clays Ltd, St Ives plc

Agatha Christie (1890-1976) is known throughout the world as the Queen of Crime. Her books have sold over a billion copies in English with another billion in over 100 foreign languages. She is the most widely published and translated author of all time and in any language; only the Bible and Shakespeare have sold more copies. She is the author of 80 crime novels and short story collections, 19 plays, and six other novels. *The Mousetrap*, her most famous play, was first staged in 1952 in London and is still performed there – it is the longest-running play in history.

Agatha Christie's first novel was published in 1920. It featured Hercule Poirot, the Belgian detective who has become the most popular detective in crime fiction since Sherlock Holmes. Collins has published Agatha Christie since 1926.

This series has been especially created for readers worldwide whose first language is not English. Each story has been shortened, and the vocabulary and grammar simplified to make it accessible to readers with a good intermediate knowledge of the language.

The following features are included after the story:

A **List of characters** to help the reader identify who is who, and how they are connected to each other. **Cultural notes** to explain historical and other references. A **Glossary** of words that some readers may not be familiar with are explained. There is also a **Recording** of the story.

Contents

Chapter 1 The Accident

Bobby Jones swung his golf club and hit his ball very hard. Did the ball fly straight and upwards? No, it did not. It raced along the ground and into the sand in the bunker! Bobby, the fourth son of the vicar of Marchbolt, a small seaside town in Wales, swore. He was a pleasant-looking young man of about twenty-eight and his eyes had the honest brown friendliness of a dog's eyes.

'I get worse every day,' he said to himself sadly.

Bobby then hit his ball really hard twice. The third time he successfully hit the ball out of the sand and it now lay a short distance from the hole he had been aiming at. His friend, Dr Thomas, a middle-aged man with a cheerful face, had reached it with two good shots.

'Well done,' said Bobby.

They went on to the next hole. The doctor went first – a nice straight shot. Bobby sighed, shut his eyes, raised his head, lowered his right shoulder – everything he should not have done – and hit a beautiful shot down the middle of the course. His sad expression changed into one of great happiness.

'I know now what I've been doing wrong,' said Bobby – quite untruthfully.

Full of confidence, he again did everything he should not have done, and this time there was no miracle. The ball went to the right instead of to the front!

'If that had been straight . . . !' said Dr Thomas with obvious relief.

'*If*,' said Bobby bitterly. 'Hello, I thought I heard a shout! I hope the ball didn't hit anyone.'

He looked to the right. But looking into the setting sun it was hard to see anything clearly and there was a mist rising from the sea. The edge of the cliff was a few hundred yards away.

'The footpath runs along there,' said Bobby, 'and I do think I heard a cry. Did you?'

The doctor had heard nothing but they walked towards the cliff edge.

Far below the sea sparkled in the sun.

'Doctor!' Bobby exclaimed. 'What do you make of that?' Twelve yards below was a pile of what looked like clothes. 'By Jove! Somebody has fallen over the cliff.'

There was a difficult path down and the two men made their way carefully to the dark pile. It was a man of about forty and he was still breathing, though unconscious. The doctor knelt to examine him. Then he looked up at Bobby and shook his head.

'He is dying, poor fellow. There is nothing I can do for him – his back is broken. Well, I suppose he wasn't familiar with the path and when the mist rose, he walked over the edge. I'll go and make arrangements to have him brought up. It's possible he may recover consciousness before the end; but very likely he won't. Will you stay?"

Bobby nodded. 'Is there really nothing that we can do for him?'

The doctor shook his head. 'Nothing, I'm afraid.'

As the doctor climbed the cliff, Bobby lit a cigarette. What terrible luck! A sudden mist, a slip – and life came to an end. Healthy-looking fellow, too, with a deep suntan. A man who had lived an out-of-door life – abroad, perhaps. Bobby studied him – the curly brown hair, the strong jaw. An attractive face . . . As he thought that, the eyes suddenly opened. They were a clear, deep blue and looked straight at Bobby.

He spoke. 'Why didn't they ask Evans?'

Then a shudder passed over him, the eyelids closed . . . The man was dead.

Chapter 2 Concerning Fathers

Sadly, Bobby took a silk handkerchief out of the dead man's pocket and put it over his face. There was nothing more he could do. Then he noticed that something else had come out of the pocket – a photograph. It was a woman's face. A fair young woman with wide-apart eyes. She seemed little more than a girl, certainly under thirty, but it was the slight sadness of her beauty rather than the beauty itself that attracted Bobby. Gently, he replaced the photograph, then sat down to wait for the doctor.

The time passed very slowly – or at least so it seemed, because he had just remembered something. He had promised to play the church organ during the six o'clock service – and it was now ten minutes to six. He wished he had sent a message with the doctor because his father was a worrier.

'He won't know whether to start the service or not,' thought Bobby, 'and he'll get so upset, he'll get stomach pain. Nobody over fifty has any sense – they worry about things that do not matter. Poor old Dad, he has got less sense than a chicken!'

He sat there thinking of his father with a mixture of affection and irritation. His life at home seemed to him to be one long sacrifice to his father's old-fashioned ideas. To Mr Jones, who was aware of how often Bobby was irritated by him, it seemed to be one long sacrifice on *his* part.

Bobby heard something above him and looked up thankfully. But it was not the doctor. It was a man whom Bobby did not know.

'I say, has there been an accident? Can I help?' He was a tall man with a pleasant voice. Bobby got up but he could not see him clearly because it was getting dark. He explained what had happened and that help was on the way – and asked if the other man could see signs of people arriving.

'No one,' the man said.

'You see,' went on Bobby, 'I have an appointment at six.'

'And you don't like to leave . . .'

'No,' said Bobby.

The other man seemed to understand. 'Look here, I'll come down and stay till help arrives.'

'Oh, would you?' said Bobby gratefully and soon the two men were face-to-face. The man was aged about thirty-five and had a rather weak face, which would have been greatly improved by a little moustache.

'My name's Bassington-ffrench. I came down to see about a house,' he explained. 'What a terrible thing to happen! Did he walk over the edge?'

Bobby nodded. 'It's a dangerous bit of path. Well, thanks very much. I've got to hurry. It's very good of you.'

'Not at all,' the other man said. 'Anybody would do the same.'

At the top of the cliff, Bobby ran. It was five minutes past six.

Chapter 3 A Railway Journey

The following morning Bobby went up to London to meet a friend who was thinking of opening a garage and who was hoping that Bobby would be working there with him.

Two days later he went to get on the 11.30 train home. The train was moving and he jumped into the first carriage he saw. It was a first-class one and the only passenger was a dark-haired girl smoking a cigarette. She had on a red skirt, a short green jacket and a little blue hat and, despite sad dark eyes, she was very good-looking.

'Why, it's you, Frankie!' Bobby said. 'I haven't seen you for ages.'

'Well, sit down and talk.'

Bobby grinned. 'My ticket is the wrong colour.'

'That doesn't matter,' said Frankie kindly. 'I'll pay the difference.'

Just then, a large figure in a blue uniform appeared. Frankie smiled at the ticket collector, who touched his hat respectfully as he took her ticket.

'Mr Jones has just come in to talk to me for a short time,' she said. 'That won't matter, will it?'

'That's all right, your ladyship.'

'What can be done with a smile,' said Bobby as the ticket collector went out.

Lady Frances Derwent shook her head thoughtfully. 'I think it's father's habit of tipping everybody really well whenever he travels that does it.'

'I thought you had given up Wales for good, Frankie.'

Frances sighed. 'After the party I went to last night, I thought even home couldn't be worse.'

'What was wrong with the party?'

'Nothing. It was just like any other party, only more so. It was to start at the Savoy at half-past eight. We had dinner and then went on to the *Marionette* club – there was a rumour it was going to be raided by the police, but nothing happened – it was just boring, and we drank a bit and then we went on to the *Bullring* nightclub and that was even more boring, and then we thought we would go and have breakfast with Angela's uncle and we were even more bored, so we went home. Honestly, Bobby, it's not good enough.'

'I suppose not,' said Bobby, resisting a feeling of jealousy. Never in his wildest moments did he dream of being able to be a member of the *Marionette* or the *Bullring*.

His relationship with Frankie Derwent was a strange one. As children, he and his brothers had played with the Derwent children at the Castle. Now they were grown up, they rarely met. On the few occasions when Frankie was at home, Bobby and his brothers would go up and play tennis. But Frankie and her two brothers were not asked to the vicarage. No one said anything about it, but it was thought that the young Derwents, who were of so much higher a social class than the Jones family, would not enjoy themselves in such simple surroundings. But Bobby was very fond of Frankie and was always pleased on the rare occasions when they met.

'I am so bored with everything,' said Frankie in a tired voice. 'Aren't you?'

'No, I don't think I am.'

'My dear, how wonderful,' said Frankie. 'By the way, what's all this about a man falling over the cliffs?'

'Dr Thomas and I found him,' said Bobby. 'How did you know about it?'

'I saw it in the paper. Look.' She pointed to a paragraph headed:

> *Fatal Accident in Sea Mist*
>
> *The victim of the tragedy at Marchbolt was identified late last night from a photograph he was carrying. The photograph proved to be that of Mrs Leo Cayman, who identified the deceased as her brother, Alex Pritchard, recently returned from Siam. He had been out of England for ten years and was just starting on a walking tour. The inquest will be held at Marchbolt tomorrow.*

'I suppose I will have to give evidence,' Bobby said.

'How exciting!'

'I don't suppose there will be anything exciting about it,' said Bobby. 'We found him – then he died about a quarter of an hour later.'

'Rather unpleasant,' said Frankie. 'Did you see the sister?'

'No. I had to see a friend of mine about a garage business we're starting up. You remember Badger Beadon? He's got funny eyes and a silly laugh – haw haw haw.'

Frankie frowned, trying to remember Badger.

'He fell off his horse when we were kids,' continued Bobby, helpfully. 'He got stuck in the mud head down and we had to pull him out by the legs.'

'Oh!' said Frankie. 'I know now. Did he also run a chicken farm which failed?'

'That's right.'

'And then they sent him to Australia and he came back?'

'Yes.'

'Bobby,' said Frankie, 'you're not putting any money into this garage business, are you?'

'I haven't got any money to put in,' said Bobby.

'Just as well,' said Frankie.

'Badger *has* tried to get hold of someone with money to put some in. But it isn't as easy as you would think.'

'When you look round you,' said Frankie, 'you would not believe people had any sense at all – but they have.'

At last Bobby understood the point of these remarks. 'Look here, Frankie,' he said. 'Badger is one of the very best.'

'They always are,' said Frankie.

'Who are?'

'The ones who go to Australia and come back again. How did he find the money to start this business?'

'An aunt died and left him a garage for six cars and his parents gave him a hundred pounds to buy second-hand cars with. You'd be surprised how cheap second-hand cars can be.'

'I bought one once,' said Frankie. 'It's a painful subject. Let's not talk of it. So, you're looking for work? What did you want to leave the Navy for?'

Bobby's face reddened. 'Eyes,' he said sadly.

'You always had trouble with your eyes, I remember.'

'I just managed to get accepted by the Navy. Then service abroad in the strong light made my eyes worse. So, well, I had to leave. It's such a shame. I could have carried on perfectly well.'

'They look all right,' said Frankie. She looked straight into his honest brown eyes.

'So you see,' said Bobby, 'I *am* going to go into business with Badger.'

It was just after five o'clock when they reached Sileham, which was the station for Marchbolt.

'Our driver's meeting me,' said Frankie. 'I'll give you a lift.'

'Thanks. That will save me carrying this thing for two miles.' He kicked his suitcase.

'It's three miles, not two,' said Frankie.

'Two miles if you go by the footpath at the edge of the golf course.'

'The one where . . .'

'Yes, where that poor man went over the edge.'

'I don't suppose someone pushed him over?' asked Frankie.

'Good Lord, no. Why?'

'Well, it would make it much more exciting, wouldn't it?' said Frankie casually.

Chapter 4 The Inquest

The inquest on Alex Pritchard was held on the following day. Dr Thomas gave evidence about the finding of the body.

'Now, as to the cause of death, Dr Thomas. There were no signs of violence that might have been made by another person?' asked the coroner.

'I can only say that the injuries are fully explained by the body hitting the rocks twelve yards below.'

'Is suicide a possibility?' questioned the coroner.

'That is perfectly possible,' said the doctor. 'But whether the dead man walked over the edge or threw himself over I cannot say.'

Bobby was called next. He explained that he had been playing golf with the doctor and had thought he had heard a cry.

The coroner asked, 'A cry for help?'

'Oh, no. Sort of surprised,' said Bobby. 'The sort of noise someone might make if a golf ball hit him unexpectedly.'

'Or if – in the mist – he took a step over the edge when he thought he was on a path?'

'Yes.'

Mrs Leo Cayman was called next. Bobby gave a gasp of disappointment. The photo from the dead man's pocket must have been taken some years ago – but even then it was hard to believe that the wide-eyed beauty in the photograph could have become this heavily made-up woman with dyed hair. Time, thought Bobby, was a very frightening thing.

Meanwhile, Amelia Cayman, of 17 St Leonard's Gardens, Paddington, London, was giving evidence. The dead man was her only brother, Alexander Pritchard, and she had last seen him the day before the tragedy.

'Did he seem in a happy and normal state of mind?'

'Oh yes. Alex was always cheerful. He was looking forward to his trip in very good spirits.'

'What was your brother's profession, Mrs Cayman?'

The lady seemed slightly embarrassed. 'Well, I can't say I really know. Prospecting – that's what he called it. He was very rarely in England.'

'You know of no reason which would cause him to take his own life?'

'Oh, no. It must have been an accident.' As she said this she began to cry.

The jury's verdict didn't take long. Death by misadventure.

Chapter 5 Mr and Mrs Cayman

On arriving back at the vicarage, Bobby found Mr and Mrs Cayman in the study with his father.

'Ah!' the vicar said. 'Here is Bobby.'

Mr Cayman rose and came towards the young man with an outstretched hand. Mr Cayman was a big, red-faced man who seemed to be friendly – but whose gaze was cold and dishonest.

'I came down with the wife,' said Mr Cayman, shaking Bobby's hand painfully hard. 'I had to support her, you know; Amelia's naturally upset.'

Mrs Cayman sniffed.

'My poor wife's brother died, I think we could say, in your arms,' continued Mr Cayman. 'Naturally, she wanted to know all you could tell her of his last moments.'

'Absolutely,' said Bobby unhappily.

'Poor, poor Alex,' said Mrs Cayman, wiping her eyes. 'If he left any last words, naturally I want to know.'

'Of course,' said Bobby. 'But he didn't.'

'It was best,' said Mr Cayman seriously, 'to pass away without pain – we should be very grateful for that, Amelia.'

'I suppose I must,' said Mrs Cayman and sighed deeply. 'Poor Alex. Such a fine man.'

'Yes, wasn't he?' said Bobby, as he accompanied the Caymans to the front door.

'And what do you do with your time, young man?' inquired Cayman.

'I spend most of my time looking for a job,' said Bobby. He paused. 'I was in the Navy.'

'Hard times – hard times these days,' said Mr Cayman, shaking his head. 'I wish you luck.'

'Thank you very much,' said Bobby politely.

As he watched them walk down the drive, various thoughts raced through his mind – the girl in the photograph's smooth pale face with the wide eyes – and fifteen years later, Mrs Cayman with all signs of youth and innocence disappeared. How sad it was! It was a result, perhaps, of marrying an obvious bounder like Cayman.

Bobby sighed and shook his head. 'That's the worst of marriage,' he said sadly.

'What did you say?'

Bobby became aware of Frankie, whose approach he had not heard.

'I was making a general comment' said Bobby. 'On the destructive effects of marriage.'

'What effects are you talking about?'

Bobby explained how badly he thought the woman had aged. He found Frankie unsympathetic.

'Nonsense. The woman's exactly like her photograph.'

'When did you see her? Were you at the inquest?'

'Of course I was at the inquest. There's so little to do down here, an inquest is a perfect gift. Of course, it would have been better if it had been a mysterious poisoning case – but one mustn't be too demanding when these simple pleasures come one's way.'

'What bloodthirsty instincts you have, Frankie. And I don't agree with you about the female Cayman. Her photograph was lovely.'

'Touched up, you know, fixed, that's all,' interrupted Frankie.

'Well, then, it was so touched up you wouldn't have known it was the same person.'

'You're blind,' said Frankie.

'Where did you see it?' Bobby demanded coldly.

'In the local *Weekly Times*.'

'It was probably badly printed.'

'It seems to me you're absolutely mad,' said Frankie crossly, 'over a painted-up, tired old bitch – yes, I said *bitch* – like Mrs Cayman.'

'Frankie,' said Bobby, 'I'm surprised at you using such bad language – and in the vicarage garden, too.'

'Well, you shouldn't be so ridiculous.'

There was a pause, then Frankie's sudden bad mood disappeared.

'What *is* ridiculous,' she said, 'is to argue about the damned woman. I came to suggest a game of golf. What about it?'

'OK, you're in charge,' said Bobby happily.

Friends again, they set off together and the recent tragedy was forgotten until Bobby, about to hit his ball, suddenly gave an exclamation.

'What is it?'

'The Caymans. They came round and asked if Pritchard had said anything before he died – and I told them he hadn't. And now I've just remembered that he did.'

'It's not one of your brightest mornings.'

'Well, it wasn't the sort of thing they meant. That's why I didn't think of it.'

'What did he say?' asked Frankie curiously.

'"*Why didn't they ask Evans*?" Then he died, poor man.'

'What a funny thing to say,' said Frankie. 'I don't understand why you're worried.'

'I just wish I'd mentioned it. You see, I told them he had said nothing at all.'

'Well, it's the same thing,' said Frankie. 'I mean, it isn't like – "Tell Gladys I always loved her", or "the will is in the wooden desk". It couldn't be important.'

'I expect you're right,' said Bobby. But he didn't feel comfortable about it, so that evening he sat down and wrote:

Dear Mr Cayman,

I have just remembered that your brother-in-law did say something before he died. The exact words were, 'Why didn't they ask Evans?' I apologize for not mentioning it this morning but I didn't think it was important at the time and so, I suppose, I just forgot.

Yours truly,
Robert Jones.

Two days later he received a reply:

Dear Mr Jones, Many thanks for repeating my poor brother-in-law's last words so carefully, in spite of their unimportance. What my wife hoped was that her brother might have left her some last message. Still, thank you for being so thorough.

Yours faithfully
Leo Cayman.

Chapter 6 End of a Picnic

On the following day Bobby received another letter:

It's all fixed, (Badger wrote). *I bought five cars yesterday for fifteen pounds the lot. At the moment they don't actually work, but we can fix them, I think. I thought of opening up a week on Monday and I am relying on you being here, so don't let me down, will you?*

Yours ever,
Badger.

Bobby told his father that he would be going up to town to take up the garage job. This did not please the vicar, who knew Badger Beadon. And then, on the Wednesday, Bobby received another letter. It was from the firm of *Henriquez and Dallo* in Buenos Aires and it offered Bobby a job with a salary of a thousand pounds a year, an unbelievable amount of money. The young man thought he must be dreaming. The letter said that an ex-Naval man was preferred for the job and Bobby's name had been put forward. His acceptance had to be immediate and Bobby must start for Buenos Aires within a week.

'Well, I'm damned!' said Bobby.

'Bobby!'

'Sorry, Dad. I forgot you were there.'

Mr Jones cleared his throat. 'I should like to point out to you . . .'

Bobby felt he had to avoid a long speech from his father. He managed to do this by making a simple statement. 'Someone's offered me a thousand a year.'

The vicar remained open-mouthed. Then he said, 'A *thousand*? It's impossible!'

Bobby was not hurt by his father's disbelief. 'They must be complete idiots,' he agreed, smiling.

'Who *are* these people?'

Bobby handed him the letter. The vicar peered at it suspiciously. 'Most remarkable.'

'Madmen!' said Bobby.

'Ah! My boy,' said the vicar, 'it is, after all, a great thing to be an Englishman. Honesty. That's what we stand for. This South American firm realizes the value of a young man who is sure to be honest.'

'But Dad,' Bobby said, 'there are a lot of Englishmen. Why me?'

'Your superior officer in the Navy may have recommended you.'

'I suppose,' said Bobby doubtfully. 'It doesn't matter, anyway, as I can't take the job.'

'My dear boy, what do you mean?'

'Well, I've taken the job with Badger.'

'Nonsense, my dear Bobby. This is serious. The garage project is a mad idea. You must give it up.'

'I can't, Sir. I've promised. I can't let Badger down. He's counting on me.'

The vicar left the room in anger and Bobby sat down to write to *Henriquez and Dallo*, refusing their offer. Later, on the golf course, he told Frankie about it.

'You would've had to go to South America?' she asked.

'Yes.'

'Would you have liked that?'

'Yes, why not?'

Frankie sighed. 'Anyway,' she said firmly, 'I think you made the right decision!'

'I couldn't let Badger down, could I?'

'No.'

They walked on in silence.

'I'm going to London tomorrow,' said Frankie.

'Tomorrow? Oh – and I was going to suggest a picnic.'

'I'd have liked that. However, it's arranged. But we can meet in London. Will you be there soon?'

'On Monday. But – well – it's no good, is it?'

'What do you mean – no good?'

'I will be working as a mechanic. And you will be with your town friends. I mean . . .'

'Bobby,' said Frankie, 'I suppose you're just as capable of coming to a cocktail party and getting drunk as any other of my friends.'

Bobby shook his head. 'Frankie, you can't mix people from different social classes.'

'I assure you,' said Frankie, 'that my friends are very mixed.'

'You're pretending not to understand.'

'You can bring Badger if you like. There's friendship for you.'

'Look here, Frankie. It's no good and you know it isn't. It's all right down here. There's not much to do and I suppose I'm better than nothing to go around with. But I know I'm just a nobody . . .'

They walked together in silence to the clubhouse.

'Well,' said Frankie, holding out her hand. 'Goodbye, my dear. It's been marvellous to have you to make use of while I've been down here. I'll see you again, perhaps, when I've nothing better to do.'

'Look, Frankie . . .'

His words were drowned in the noise of the Bentley's engine which Frankie had just started. She drove away with a wave of her hand.

'Damn!' said Bobby. Perhaps he hadn't explained things very well, but what he had said was true. Perhaps, though, he shouldn't have put it into words.

★ ★ ★

The next three days seemed very, very long. The vicar was silently disapproving of Bobby's decision to go and work for Badger, and on Saturday Bobby could stand it no longer. He got Mrs Roberts, the vicarage cook, to give him some sandwiches, and, buying a bottle of beer at the pub, he set off alone for a picnic. He had missed Frankie badly these last few days.

Bobby walked a few miles, then, feeling tired and hungry, he stretched himself out on the ground and wondered whether he should eat his lunch first and go to sleep afterwards, or sleep first and eat afterwards. The decision was made for him because he fell asleep without noticing it. When he awoke it was half-past three, so he ate his lunch hungrily. With a sigh of satisfaction he unscrewed the bottle of beer. Unusually bitter beer, but refreshing . . .

He lay back down, suddenly tired again. Sleep overcame him. Heavy, endless sleep.

Chapter 7 An Escape from Death

Frankie's Bentley stopped outside a large, old-fashioned house. She jumped out and, turning, lifted a large bunch of expensive flowers from the back seat, then turned again and rang the doorbell. A nurse answered the door.

'Can I see Mr Jones?' inquired Frankie.

The nurse looked at the Bentley, the flowers and Frankie with interest. 'What name will I say?'

'Lady Frances Derwent.'

The nurse was thrilled – a Lady! Her patient must be more important than she thought! She showed Frankie upstairs into a room on the first floor.

'You've a visitor to see you, Mr Jones.'

'Gosh!' said Bobby, very much surprised. 'Frankie!'

'Hello, Bobby, I've brought flowers that are more usually seen at a funeral, but the choice was limited.'

'Oh, Lady Frances,' said the nurse, 'they're lovely. I'll put them into water.' She left the room.

Frankie sat down in a visitor's chair. 'Well, Bobby,' she said. 'What's all this?'

'You may well ask,' said Bobby. 'My body took in eight grains of morphia, no less. They're going to write about me in *The British Medical Journal.* Do you know, my girl, that half a grain of morphia is a fatal quantity? I ought to be dead sixteen times over. It's true that recovery has been known after sixteen grains – still, eight is pretty good, don't you think? This nursing home has never had a case like me before.'

'How nice for them.'

'Isn't it? You'll see, I will be famous,' he said and began telling Frankie every detail of his treatment.

'That's enough,' said Frankie, stopping him. 'I don't want to hear about how stomach pumps work. And to listen to you, one would think nobody had ever been poisoned before.'

'Very few people have been poisoned with eight grains of morphia and got over it,' Bobby pointed out. 'Really, Frankie, you're not impressed enough.'

'It must be very annoying for the people who poisoned you,' said Frankie.

'I know. What a waste of perfectly good morphia.'

'It was in the beer, wasn't it?'

'Yes. They analysed the drops of beer left in the bottle. You see, someone found me sleeping like the dead and got frightened. He carried me to a farmhouse, and sent for a doctor.'

'Is there any clue as to how the morphia got in the bottle?' Frankie asked.

'None. They've opened other bottles at the pub where I bought it and everything's all right.'

'Then someone must have put the stuff in the beer while you were asleep?'

'That's it.'

Frankie nodded thoughtfully. 'Well,' she said. 'That decides it. That man – Alex Pritchard – *was* pushed over the cliff.'

'*What*?' said Bobby, surprised.

'Darling – it's obvious. Why should anyone want to kill *you*? You're not the heir to a fortune. No one benefits by your death. There's revenge, of course. You haven't seduced a chemist's daughter, have you?'

'Not that I can remember,' said Bobby.

'I know. One seduces so many people that one can't keep count. But I would guess that you've never seduced anyone at all.'

'You're making me embarrassed, Frankie. And why must it be a chemist's daughter?'

'She would have free access to morphia. It's not so easy to get hold of morphia.'

'Well, I haven't seduced a chemist's daughter.'

'And you haven't got any enemies that you know of?'

Bobby shook his head.

'Well,' said Frankie, 'what do the police think?'

'They think it must have been a madman.'

'Nonsense. Madmen don't wander about with morphia looking for bottles of beer to put it into. No, somebody pushed Pritchard over the cliff. A minute or two later you came along and the murderer thought you saw something that you didn't think was anything but which really was something. That sounds confused, but it's really logical. If you get two strange things happening in a quiet place like Marchbolt – wait – there's a third thing.'

'What?'

'That job you were offered. It was strange, you must admit. You can see what I'm thinking. They first try to get rid of you by offering you a job abroad. Then, when that fails, they try to kill you.'

'Isn't that rather extreme?'

'Oh! But murderers are *very* extreme.'

'Well, Frankie, what on earth am I supposed to have seen?'

'That is the question,' admitted Frankie, getting up from the chair. 'I don't know! Shall I come and see you again tomorrow?'

'Please do. By the way, you're back from London very soon, aren't you.'

'My dear, as soon as I heard about you, I raced back. It's most exciting to have a romantically poisoned friend. Well, I'll come tomorrow. Do I kiss you or don't I?'

'It's not catching,' said Bobby encouragingly.

'Then I'll do my duty to the sick thoroughly.' She kissed him lightly.

The nurse came in with Bobby's tea as Frankie went out.

'Isn't she nice?' the nurse said. 'Not a bit haughty, is she?'

'Oh, no!' said Bobby. 'I should never call Frankie haughty.'

'I said to Sister, I said, she's as natural as anything. Not a bit as you would think a Lady would be. I said to Sister, she's just like you or me, I said.'

Silently disagreeing violently from this view, Bobby made no reply. The nurse, disappointed by his lack of response, left the room.

Left to his own thoughts, Bobby went over in his mind the possibilities of Frankie's amazing theory. He decided – reluctantly, as it made him feel important – against it. With a sigh he picked up the previous week's *Marchbolt Weekly Times*. A moment later he pressed the emergency bell and a nurse came running.

'Ring up the Castle,' cried Bobby. 'Tell Lady Frances she must come back at once!'

★ ★ ★

'What do you want to see me about so urgently?' Frankie demanded.

Bobby waved the *Marchbolt Weekly Times*. 'Look, Frankie. This is the picture you said was touched up.'

Underneath a somewhat blurred photograph were the words: 'PHOTOGRAPH FOUND ON THE DEAD MAN AND BY WHICH HE WAS IDENTIFIED. MRS AMELIA CAYMAN, THE DEAD MAN'S SISTER.'

'That's what I said – and it's true.'

'No. You see, Frankie – *this isn't the photograph that I put back in the dead man's pocket.*'

'That man who stayed with him – what's his name?' said Frankie.

'Bassington-ffrench!' said Bobby. 'He must have exchanged them.'

Chapter 8 Mystery of a Photograph

They stared at each other.

'It couldn't be anyone else,' said Bobby. 'He was the only person who *could* have taken one photograph away and put another in its place.'

'What was this Bassington-ffrench like, Bobby?'

Bobby frowned in the effort of remembering. 'Very ordinary. Pleasant voice. A gentleman. I really didn't notice him particularly. He said something about looking for a house.'

'We can check that,' said Frankie. '*Wheeler & Owen* are the only house agents.' Suddenly she shivered, 'Bobby, if Pritchard was pushed over the cliff, *Bassington-ffrench must be the man who pushed him.* Everything fits. Your unexpected appearance spoilt the murderer's plans. Your discovery of the photograph and, as a result, the need to get rid of you.'

'There's a problem there,' said Bobby. 'Let's say that the photograph was so important I had to be "got out of the way". Then it would have to be done *at once.* The fact that I went to London and never saw the photograph in the *Marchbolt Weekly Times* was pure chance. Otherwise I would have immediately said: "That isn't the photograph I saw." Why wait till after the inquest when everything was nicely settled and no one had any idea that Pritchard had been murdered?'

'It must have been something else,' admitted Frankie. 'Something they didn't know about till after the inquest. Bobby, what was it Pritchard said, just before he died?'

'"*Why didn't they ask Evans*?"'

'Suppose *that* was it? Bobby, I'm *sure* it's that. Oh, no, I'm being an idiot – you never told the Caymans about it!'

'I did,' said Bobby slowly. 'I wrote to them that evening.'

'And two days later you got this letter asking you to go to South America?'

'Yes.'

'Well,' said Frankie, 'you turn it down – and the next thing – they poured morphia into your bottle of beer.'

'According to our present theory,' Bobby said thoughtfully, 'it goes like this. Dead man X – because we don't know that his name really is Pritchard – is pushed over the cliff. It is important that X should not be identified, so a portrait of Mrs C is put in his pocket and the portrait of the beautiful girl removed. Who was she, I wonder?'

'Keep to the point,' said Frankie, irritated.

'Mrs C waits for the photograph to appear and then, pretending to be the very sad sister, identifies X as her brother who has just returned from abroad,' said Bobby.

'You don't believe he could really have been her brother?'

'Not for a moment! You know, it puzzled me all along. The Caymans were a different class altogether. The dead man was – well, it sounds a most awful thing to say and so old-fashioned, but the dead man was definitely from the upper classes.'

'And the Caymans most emphatically weren't?'

'*Most* emphatically.'

'And then, just when everything has gone well from the Caymans' point of view – you mess things up,' said Frankie.

'"*Why didn't they ask Evans*?"' Bobby repeated. 'I can't see what on earth there can be in that to make anyone anxious.'

'Well, the question must have meant something really important to them – and they couldn't have realized it meant nothing to you. But they weren't going to take a chance. You were safer out of the way.'

'They took a lot of risk. Why didn't they plan another "accident"?'

'No, no. That would have been stupid. Two accidents within a week of each other? It might have suggested a connection between the two, and then people would have begun another investigation of the first one.'

'And yet you said that morphia wasn't easy to get.'

'It isn't. You have to sign poison books and things. Oh! Of course, that's a clue. Whoever did it had easy access to supplies of morphia.'

'A doctor, a hospital nurse, or a chemist,' suggested Bobby.

'Well, I was thinking more of illegally imported drugs.'

'You can't mix up too many different sorts of crime,' said Bobby.

'But the strong point would be the absence of motive,' said Frankie. 'Your death doesn't benefit anyone. So what will the police think?'

'A madman,' said Bobby. 'And that's what the police actually do think.'

'You see? It's very simple, really.'

Bobby began to laugh suddenly.

'What's amusing you?'

'Just the thought of how sickening it must be for them! All that morphia – enough to kill sixteen people – and here I am, still alive and well. But the question is – what do we do next?'

'Oh! Lots of things,' said Frankie immediately.

'Such as . . .?'

'We find out about Bassington-ffrench's house hunting,' said Frankie. 'If he even did any.'

'He will have. Think for a minute. Bassington-ffrench *must* be above suspicion. Not only must there be nothing to connect him with the dead man, there must be no suggestion of a "mysterious stranger seen in the neighbourhood of the accident."'

'Yes,' said Frankie thoughtfully. 'Now, if we knew who the dead man really was . . .'

'It was certainly important that he shouldn't be recognized – which was why there was all the pretence of Mrs Cayman being his sister,' Bobby said. 'After that, even if there *had* been pictures of him in the papers, people would only say: "Isn't it strange, this man Pritchard, who fell over a cliff, is really incredibly like Mr X."'

'And he couldn't have been a family man whose wife or relations would go to the police at once and report him missing,' said Frankie wisely.

'Perhaps he *had* just come back from abroad, Frankie. He was marvellously suntanned – like a big-game hunter.'

'"*Why didn't they ask Evans*?"' Frankie said. 'The dead man must have come down here to see Evans. Now, if we could find Evans . . .'

'How many Evanses,' Bobby interrupted, 'do you think there are in Marchbolt?'

'Seven hundred, I should think,' admitted Frankie. 'At least!'

'So, it's Bassington-ffrench we must investigate,' Frankie decided.

'There we *have* got something solid to go on. It's an uncommon name. I'll ask Father. He knows the names of most of the aristocratic families and where they live.'

'Yes,' Bobby said, 'that's a good idea. Then we might do something.'

'We *are* going to do something, aren't we?'

'Of course we are. Do you think I'm going to be given eight grains of morphia and do nothing about it?'

'That's the spirit,' said Frankie.

'And besides that,' said Bobby, 'there's the unpleasant experience of having the morphia pumped out of my stomach.'

'That's enough,' said Frankie. 'You'll be giving me all the horrible details again if I don't stop you.'

'And I thought women were supposed to be the sympathetic sex!' said Bobby.

Chapter 9 Concerning Mr Bassington-ffrench

'Father,' Frankie said that evening, 'do you know any Bassington-ffrenches?'

'What about them?' said Lord Marchington.

Frankie didn't know anything about them. She made a statement, knowing that her father enjoyed disagreement. 'They're a Yorkshire family, aren't they?'

'Nonsense – they're from Hampshire. There's the Shropshire ones, of course, and the Irish lot. Which are your friends?'

'I'm not sure,' said Frankie. 'People move around so much nowadays. Are they well off?'

'I couldn't say. The Shropshire lot have lost a lot of their money, I believe. One of the Hampshire ones married an heiress. An American woman.'

* * *

On the following day Frankie walked into the office of *Wheeler & Owen, House and Estate Agents*. Mr Owen himself jumped up to receive her. Frankie gave him a surprisingly friendly smile and dropped into a chair.

'And what can we have the pleasure of doing for you, Lady Frances?'

'I believe a friend of mine was down here the other day – a Mr Bassington-ffrench.'

'Ah! Yes, indeed. He was making inquiries about small properties because he would like to buy a house here. But he had to return to town the next day. I have sent him the information on one or two.'

'Did you write to London – or to the country address?' inquired Frankie.

'Frank!' He called to a young clerk. 'Mr Bassington-ffrench's address.'

'Merroway Court, Staverley, Hampshire,' said the clerk.

'Ah!' said Frankie. 'Then it wasn't *my* Mr Bassington-ffrench. This must be his cousin. I thought it was odd his being here and not contacting me.'

Frankie left the office in a thoughtful mood. Mr Bassington-ffrench seemed clear and honest – but no, she decided, Bassington-ffrench *was* the guilty person, and began to make plans.

Chapter 10 Preparations for an Accident

A week later Bobby had joined Badger in London. Frankie wrote that she had a plan and he was to do nothing until he heard from her. This was welcome advice, since Bobby was kept busy undoing the mess that Badger had already made of the business. Meanwhile, the effect of being given eight grains of morphia was making Bobby extremely suspicious of food and drink and had also persuaded him to bring to London a gun which he'd got in the Navy. He was just beginning to feel that the whole thing had simply been a nightmare when Frankie's Bentley finally stopped outside the garage. Frankie was driving and beside her sat a rather gloomy-looking young man.

'Hello, Bobby,' said Frankie. 'This is George Arbuthnot. He's a doctor, and we shall need him.'

'Aren't you being a bit pessimistic?' Bobby asked.

'Look here,' said Frankie. 'I've got everything planned. We want a car to crash and one of yours will do.'

'She means,' George Arbuthnot said, 'that she's going to have an accident.'

'How does she know?' said Bobby wildly.

Frankie gave an annoyed sigh. 'Now just listen, Bobby. Bassington-ffrench lives at Merroway Court at Staverley in Hampshire – which belongs to his brother – with his brother and his wife.'

'Who's wife?'

'The brother's wife! I've made a plan: Lady Frances Derwent, driving her car dangerously, crashes into the wall near the gates of Merroway Court. Lady Frances is carried to the house, suffering from concussion and shock and must not be moved for two or three days.'

'Who says so?'

'George. George is passing; sees the accident, jumps out of his car, makes his examination, says what's wrong with her, and goes away.'

'And where do I come in?' Bobby asked.

'You don't. My dear child, Bassington-ffrench has met you already, but he doesn't know me. But I am a Lady and therefore *highly* respectable. And George is a *real* doctor so everything is quite above suspicion.'

'And I don't do anything at all?' asked Bobby. He felt like a dog whose bone has been taken away.

'Of course you do, darling. You grow a moustache.'

'Oh! Do I? Once I've got the moustache, what do I do?'

'Put on a chauffeur's uniform and drive the Bentley down to Staverley.'

Bobby looked more cheerful.

'Nobody looks at a chauffeur in the way they look at a *person*,' said Frankie. 'I'd bet anything that seeing you in a chauffeur's uniform with a moustache, Bassington-ffrench wouldn't recognise you. Now tell me, what do you think of the plan?'

'It's pretty good,' Bobby said generously.

'In that case,' said Frankie briskly, 'let's buy a car.'

They entered the garage, where a young man with an agreeable smile greeted them with a rather silly laugh: 'Haw, haw, haw!'

'Hello, Badger,' said Bobby. 'You remember Frankie, don't you?'

Badger clearly didn't, but he said, 'Haw, haw, haw!' again in a friendly way.

'Frankie wants to buy a car,' said Bobby.

'Well, come and look at what we've got in stock,' said Badger.

'They look very smart,' said Frankie, amazed by their extremely bright colours.

'That Chrysler is very good value,' said Badger.

'No,' said Bobby. 'Whatever she buys has got to go at least forty miles an hour.'

Badger looked at his partner unhappily.

'The Standard isn't wonderful,' said Bobby. 'But I think it would just get you there.'

'All right,' said Frankie. 'I'll have the Standard.'

Badger took Bobby to one side. 'What do you think about the price?' he whispered. 'I don't want to charge a friend of yours too much. Ten pounds?'

'Ten pounds is all right,' said Frankie. 'I'll pay for it now.'

'Who is she really?' asked Badger in a loud whisper.

Bobby whispered back.

'First time I ever knew anyone with a title who is prepared to pay cash,' said Badger with respect. 'They usually expect to put everything on an account.'

Chapter 11 The Accident Happens

The place Frankie had selected for the accident was half a mile after the Staverley turn off from the main road.

'It couldn't be better,' she said. 'Straight down this hill and then the road makes a sharp turn. If we let the car run down the hill, it will crash straight into the wall and something terrible ought to happen to it.'

'It should,' Bobby agreed. 'But someone ought to be watching at the corner.'

'Quite right,' said Frankie. 'We don't want to involve anybody else. George can take his car down and turn it as though he were coming from the other direction. When he waves, it will show that all is clear.'

'You're looking very pale, Frankie,' said Bobby anxiously. 'Are you all right?'

'I've got pale make-up on,' explained Frankie. 'Ready for the concussion.'

'You'll – look after yourself, won't you?' said Bobby with a sudden seriousness. 'I mean, don't go and do anything foolish.'

'I shall be extremely careful. I'll write a letter to my maid to bring to you when I want you to come down.'

'I'll get busy with the moustache. See you later, Frankie.'

They looked at each other for a moment and then Frankie nodded and walked down the hill. George had turned the car. A handkerchief waved at the corner. Bobby leaned into the car and released the brake. The car moved forward, the engine started, then the car went on down the hill and crashed into the wall. Bobby saw Frankie get into the wreckage. With a sigh he got on his motorcycle and rode away in the direction of London.

At the scene of the accident things were busy.

'Shall I roll about a bit,' asked Frankie, 'to get myself dusty?'

'You might as well,' said George. 'No, lie still, I heard a bicycle bell.'

Sure enough, at that moment, a boy of about seventeen came whistling round the corner. He stopped at once, delighted with the sight that met his eyes.

'Oh!' he said, 'Has there been an accident?'

'No,' said George sarcastically. 'The young lady ran her car into the wall on purpose.'

'Looks bad, doesn't it?' the boy said happily. 'Is she dead?'

'Not yet,' said George. 'She must be taken somewhere at once. I'm a doctor. What's this place in here?'

'Merroway Court. It belongs to Mr Bassington-ffrench.'

'She must be carried there at once,' said George authoritatively.

Between them they carried Frankie up the drive to a pleasant manor house. An elderly butler came out to meet them.

'There's been an accident,' said George curtly. 'Is there a room I can carry this lady into?'

A woman appeared. She was tall, with red hair and was about thirty years of age. Her eyes were a light clear blue. 'There is a spare bedroom on the ground floor,' she said in a cool voice with a slight American accent. 'Will you bring her in there? Ought I to telephone for a doctor?'

'I *am* a doctor,' explained George. 'I was passing and saw the accident.'

'Oh! How fortunate. Come this way, will you?' She showed them into a pleasant bedroom with windows on to the garden. 'Is she badly hurt?' she inquired.

'I can't tell yet.'

Mrs Bassington-ffrench took the hint and left the room. George studied his watch and finally said, with relief, 'Time.'

'George, darling,' said Frankie, 'you've been an angel.'

George went in search of Mrs Bassington-ffrench, whom he found in the drawing-room.

'Well,' he said, 'she has very slight concussion but she ought to stay quietly where she is for a day or so.' He paused. 'She seems to be a Lady Frances Derwent.'

'Oh!' said Mrs Bassington-ffrench. 'I know some cousins of hers – the Draycotts – quite well.'

'I don't know if it's inconvenient for you to have her here,' said George. 'But if she could stay . . .'

'Oh, of course. That will be all right, Dr . . .?'

'Arbuthnot. By the way, I'll be passing a garage. I'll get them to see to her car.'

'Thank you very much, Dr Arbuthnot. How very lucky you happened to be passing. I suppose a doctor ought to see her tomorrow just to see she's getting on all right.'

'Oh, I don't think it's necessary,' said George. 'All she needs is quiet. You can take my word for it.'

'If you really think so, Dr Arbuthnot,' said Mrs Bassington-ffrench.

Chapter 12 In the Enemy's Camp

Frankie spent a dull afternoon and evening lying in her room with the curtains closed. The next day she opened them to let the daylight in and her hostess came and sat with her. They discovered they knew many of the same people and by the end of the day, Frankie felt, a little guiltily, that they had become friends. Mrs Bassington-ffrench seemed a simple woman, very fond of her home, and yet Frankie felt that she was not quite happy.

On the third day Frankie left her room and was introduced to the master of the house. He was a big man, pleasant but a bit distant – and had rather strange eyes, Frankie thought. He seemed to spend a lot of his time working in his study. Tommy, their small boy, was seven, and a healthy, energetic child. Sylvia Bassington-ffrench obviously adored him.

'It's so nice down here,' said Frankie with a sigh. She was lying out on a long chair in the garden. 'I don't know whether it's the bang on the head, or what, but I'd like to lie here for days and days.'

'Well, do,' said Sylvia Bassington-ffrench. 'It's a great pleasure to me to have you here. You're so bright and amusing – it cheers me up.'

Frankie felt ashamed of herself.

'I feel we really have become friends,' continued the other woman. Frankie felt still more ashamed. It was a mean thing she was doing – mean.

Her hostess went on, 'It won't be too boring here. Tomorrow my brother-in-law is coming back. You'll like him, I'm sure. Everyone likes Roger.'

'Does he live with you?'

'Sometimes. He never sticks to a job for long – in fact, I don't believe he's ever done any real work in his life. But some people just are like that – especially in old families. And Roger is wonderfully sympathetic. I don't know what I would have done without him this spring when Tommy was ill.'

'What was wrong with Tommy?'

'He fell from the swing when the branch Roger had tied its ropes onto broke. Roger was very upset because he felt responsible and we thought at first Tommy's back was badly hurt, but he's quite all right now.'

'He certainly looks it,' said Frankie, smiling, as she heard him playing noisily in the distance.

'I know. It's such a relief. He's had bad luck in accidents. He was nearly drowned last winter.'

'Was he really?' said Frankie thoughtfully. The feeling of guilt had gone. Accidents! Did Roger Bassington-ffrench specialize in accidents, she wondered. She said, 'If you're sure, I'd love to stay a little longer. But won't your husband mind?'

'Henry?' Mrs Bassington-ffrench's face looked sad, suddenly. 'No, Henry won't mind. Henry never minds anything – nowadays.'

Henry Bassington-ffrench joined them for tea and Frankie studied him closely. There was certainly something strange about the man. His type was an obvious one – a sociable, sport-loving country gentleman. But such a man ought not to walk about nervously or sit in thoughts so deep that he seemed completely unaware of anyone else's presence, as now, or make bitter and sarcastic replies to anything said to him. Later, at dinner, he joked, laughed, told stories and was quite brilliant. Too brilliant, Frankie felt. The brilliance was just as unnatural and out of character.

'He has such strange eyes,' Frankie thought. 'They frighten me a little.'

★ ★ ★

Roger Bassington-ffrench arrived on the following afternoon and they met on the grass where tea was laid.

'This is my brother-in-law,' Sylvia said smiling. 'Lady Frances Derwent.'

They shook hands. Frankie saw a tall, slim, very pleasant young man with deep blue eyes. He said, 'I've been hearing all about the way you tried to break down the park wall.'

'I was driving an awful old car,' said Frankie. 'My own needed some repairs and I bought a cheap one, second-hand.'

Tommy arrived at this moment and threw himself upon his uncle with shouts of joy. Frankie watched them, feeling confused. Surely this charming young man couldn't be a cold-blooded murderer!

But then who had pushed Pritchard over the cliff? And there was still the matter of the changed photograph. And who had put the morphia in Bobby's beer? With the thought of morphia, suddenly the explanation came to Frankie, of Henry Bassington-ffrench's eyes with their tiny <u>pupils</u>. Was Henry Bassington-ffrench *a drug <u>addict</u>?*

Chapter 13 Alan Carstairs

Strangely enough, Frankie's theory was confirmed the following day. She and Roger had been playing tennis and were sitting afterwards sipping iced drinks. Talking about various subjects, Frankie had become more and more aware of the charm of someone who had, like Roger, travelled all over the world. A pause was broken by Roger – and in an entirely different tone from the light-hearted one he'd been using.

'Lady Frances, I've known you less than twenty-four hours, but I feel that you're the one person I can ask advice from.' He paused again. He looked worried and upset. 'It's about my brother – his extreme changes of mood. He is taking drugs, I am sure of it. Have you noticed his eyes? The pupils are very small.'

'I have,' admitted Frankie. 'What do you think it is?'

'Morphia. I think it comes to him in the afternoon post. You'll have noticed how his mood changes between tea and dinner.'

'Has it been going on for long?'

'About six months. The thing is, I don't know if I should tell Sylvia. That's why I thought you might be able to help me. Sylvia likes you a lot. What should I do, Lady Frances? If I tell her, I will worry her terribly.'

'If she knew, she might have some influence,' suggested Frankie.

'I doubt it. When it's drug taking, nobody has any influence. No, I've been thinking that Henry might be prepared to go away for treatment if Sylvia didn't know – if her knowing was used as a threat.'

'Would he have to go away?'

'No. There's actually a place about three miles from here. Run by a Dr Nicholson – a Canadian. A very clever man. And, fortunately, Henry likes him. Hush – here comes Sylvia!'

Mrs Bassington-ffrench joined them, saying, 'Have you played much tennis?'

'We played one game,' said Frankie.

'We must ask the Nicholsons over,' said Sylvia. 'She's very fond of tennis. Why – what is it?' She had seen the glance the other two had exchanged.

'Nothing – only I happened to be talking about the Nicholsons to Lady Frances.'

'They are Canadians, aren't they?' inquired Frankie.

'He is. I think that she is English. She's a very pretty little thing – quite charming, with the most lovely big, slightly sad, eyes. I think she isn't very happy.'

'He runs a kind of sanatorium, a nursing home, doesn't he?'

'Yes – nerve cases and people who take drugs. He's very successful, I believe. He's rather an impressive man.'

'Do you like him?'

'No,' said Sylvia, 'I don't.'

Later on, she pointed out to Frankie a photograph which stood on the piano.

'That's Moira Nicholson. A lovely face, isn't it? A man who came down here with friends of ours some time ago was quite attracted by it. He wanted an introduction, I think.' She laughed. 'I'll ask them to dinner tomorrow night. I'd like to know what you think of him. I dislike him – and yet he's quite attractive looking.'

Something in her tone made Frankie look at her quickly, but Sylvia had turned away.

'It's time I asked some questions,' Frankie thought, making up her mind.

★ ★ ★

She began fairly naturally at dinner. 'You know,' she said to Roger, 'I can't help feeling that we've met before. It wasn't, by any chance, at that party of Lady Shane's at *Claridges*. On the 16th?'

'It couldn't have been on the 16th,' said Sylvia quickly. 'Roger was here. We had a children's party that day and what I would have done without Roger, I simply don't know.'

She gave a grateful glance at her brother-in-law and he smiled back at her. '

'I'm sure if I had met you before, I'd remember it,' Roger said.

One point settled, thought Frankie. Roger Bassington-ffrench was not in Wales on the day Bobby was poisoned.

'Strangely enough, that was the day a man fell over the cliff in our neighbourhood. I went home a few days later and I went to the inquest, thinking it would be exciting.'

'Was that at Marchbolt?' asked Sylvia.

Frankie nodded. 'Derwent Castle is only about seven miles from Marchbolt,' she explained.

'Roger, that must have been your man,' cried Sylvia.

Frankie looked inquiringly at him.

'I was actually there,' said Roger. 'I stayed with the body till the police came.'

'How perfectly extraordinary!' said Frankie.

There was a general atmosphere of 'How strange! Isn't the world small?' Frankie felt she was doing this rather well.

'Roger had some silly idea of buying a house down there,' said Sylvia.

'Complete rubbish,' said Henry Bassington-ffrench. 'You know perfectly well, Roger, that as soon as you'd bought it, you'd get bored staying in one place and go off abroad again.'

Roger laughed. Then he turned to Frankie. '*Was* there anything interesting or exciting at the inquest?'

'Oh, no, it was all boringly straightforward and some unpleasant relations came and identified the man. He was on a walking tour, it seems. It was very sad, really, because he was extremely good looking. Did you see his picture in the papers?'

'I did,' said Sylvia. 'He looked very like that man, Alan Carstairs. I remember saying so at the time.'

'Yes,' agreed Roger. 'He did look like him – in that photograph.'

'You can't tell from newspaper pictures, can you?' said Sylvia.

Everyone, it seemed to Frankie, had reacted with perfect naturalness. The only thing she had succeeded in was getting a name. Alan Carstairs.

Chapter 14 Dr Nicholson

Frankie said to Sylvia the following morning, 'That man you mentioned last night. Alan Carstairs. I feel sure I've heard that name before.'

'I expect you have. He's rather a celebrity. He's a Canadian – an explorer. Some friends of ours, the Rivingtons, brought him down one day for lunch. A very attractive man – big and suntanned and with nice blue eyes. Last year he went on a tour through Africa with that millionaire, John Savage – the one who thought he had cancer and killed himself in that sad way . . .'

Frankie was convinced that Alan Carstairs had been the victim at Marchbolt. But to show too much interest would be fatal. Inquiries must be discreet.

'I don't want to be poisoned,' thought Frankie with a frown.

That evening, Dr Nicholson and his wife were expected to dinner. Carstairs had been a Canadian. Dr Nicholson was a Canadian. Madness to build anything upon that, of course, but wasn't it just too much of a coincidence?

* * *

Dr Nicholson was a big man with a manner that suggested great power. His speech was slow and he said very little that evening, but somehow he made every word sound important. He wore strong glasses and behind them his pale-blue eyes seemed very large. His wife was a slim and delicate creature of perhaps twenty-seven, pretty, indeed beautiful. She seemed, Frankie thought, nervous and chattered too quickly.

'You had an accident, I hear, Lady Frances,' said Dr Nicholson as he took his seat beside her at the dinner table.

Frankie explained what had happened. She wondered why she should feel so nervous doing so. There was no reason for him to suspect that she had staged the accident.

'That was too bad,' he said, as she finished. 'But you seem to have made a very good recovery.'

'We won't admit she's cured yet. We're keeping her with us,' said Sylvia.

The doctor's gaze went to Sylvia. 'I should keep her with you as long as possible,' he said very seriously.

Frankie was sitting between her host and Dr Nicholson. Henry Bassington-ffrench was very moody tonight. His hands shook, he ate almost nothing and took no part in the conversation. Mrs Nicholson had a difficult time with him and turned to Roger with obvious relief. But Frankie noticed that her eyes went to her husband's face frequently.

Dr Nicholson turned to Frankie again. 'I had heard of your accident, you know. One thing about it bothered me.'

'Yes?' said Frankie, her heart beating fast suddenly.

'The doctor who was passing – the one who brought you in here.'

'Yes?'

'He must have had a strange character – to turn his car before going to the rescue.'

'I don't understand.'

'Of course not. You were unconscious. But young Reeves, the message boy who accompanied you here, came from Staverley on his bicycle and no car passed him, yet he came round the corner, found the crash, and the doctor's car pointing the same way he was going – towards London. You see the point? The doctor did not come from Staverley, so he must have come the other way, down the hill. Therefore he must have turned his car.'

The pale blue eyes were staring at her through the thick glasses.

'You sound like a detective, Jasper,' said Mrs Nicholson. 'And all about nothing at all.'

'Little things interest me,' said Nicholson.

He turned to his hostess and Frankie took a breath of relief. It seemed to her that Dr Nicholson was an evil man. She kept out of his way after dinner, staying close to the gentle, delicate Mrs Nicholson. She noticed that all the time Mrs Nicholson's eyes still watched her husband. Was it love, Frankie wondered, or fear? Nicholson devoted himself to Sylvia and at half-past ten he must have made a secret sign to his wife for they got up to leave at the same moment.

'Well,' said Roger after they had gone, 'what do you think of our Dr Nicholson? He has a very strong personality, hasn't he?'

'I'm like Sylvia,' said Frankie. 'I don't like *him* very much. I like her better.'

'Good-looking, but rather a little idiot,' said Roger. 'She either adores him or is scared to death of him – I don't know which.'

'That's just what I wondered,' agreed Frankie.

'I don't like him,' said Sylvia, 'but I must admit he's got a lot of – of *power.* I believe he's cured drug takers in the most marvellous way. People whose relations had become really desperate. They've gone there as a last hope and come out absolutely cured.'

'Yes,' cried Henry Bassington-ffrench suddenly. 'And do you know what goes on there? Do you know the pain he suffers?

A man gets used to a drug, but they take it away from him suddenly – and he goes mad because he doesn't have it and beats his head against the wall. That's what he does – your "powerful" doctor tortures people!'

He was shaking violently. Suddenly he turned and left the room. Sylvia looked shocked. 'What is the matter with Henry?' she asked.

Frankie and Roger dared not look at each other. Before she went to sleep that night, Frankie wrote to Bobby.

Chapter 15 A Discovery

It was just after tea that the Bentley came up the drive of Merroway Court, a young and correct chauffeur at the wheel. Frankie went out to the front door. Sylvia and Roger came with her.

'Is everything all right, Hawkins?'

The chauffeur, who was, of course, Bobby in disguise, complete with moustache, touched his cap respectfully. 'Yes, M'lady. The Bentley's been completely repaired.' He produced a note. 'From his lordship, M'lady.'

Frankie took it. 'You will stay at the *Angler's Arms* in Staverley, Hawkins. I'll telephone in the morning.'

'Very good, your ladyship.' Bobby turned and drove quickly down the drive.

'It's a lovely car,' said Sylvia.

'You get some speed out of that,' said Roger.

'I do,' admitted Frankie.

She was satisfied that Roger hadn't recognised Bobby. She would have been surprised if he had. The uniform, the moustache and the formal behaviour, so uncharacteristic of Bobby, made him a very different man from the one Roger had met beside the body on the cliff side. The voice, too, had been excellent.

Meanwhile, Bobby had settled into his room at the *Angler's Arms* and successfully created the part of Edward Hawkins, chauffeur to Lady Frances Derwent. Bobby knew nothing of the behaviour of chauffeurs in private life, but he imagined that an amount of superiority would be right. The young women employed at the *Angler's Arms* quickly showed that they clearly admired him, which made him feel he was doing well in his disguise, and he soon found that Frankie and her accident had provided the main topic of conversation in Staverley ever since it had happened.

Frankie's letter had asked Bobby to get any local information he could, so he spoke to the pub landlord, a round, friendly person called Thomas Askew.

'Very nice little place you have here, Mr Askew,' said Bobby, managing to be both superior and kindly. 'Very nice and comfortable.'

Mr Askew looked pleased.

'Is Merroway Court the only big place in the neighbourhood?'

'Well, there's the Grange, Mr Hawkins. It has been empty for years until this American doctor took it. Nicholson his name is. And if you ask me, Mr Hawkins, there are some very strange things happening there.'

The barmaid at this point remarked that Dr Nicholson frightened her a bit.

'What strange things, Mr Askew?' said Bobby.

Mr Askew shook his head sadly. 'Many of the patients there don't want to be. They've been put into the Grange by their relations. They are people who have had breakdowns, for instance. And they can't get out without their relations' permission. I assure you, Mr Hawkins, you wouldn't believe the screams and groans that go on there.'

Here the barmaid joined in eagerly. 'Why, one night a poor young woman escaped – in her nightgown she was – and the doctor and a couple of nurses were out looking for her. "Oh! don't let them take me back!" she was crying out. It was so sad. She said that she was rich and that her relations had put her away. But the people at the Grange took her back, they did, and the doctor explained she'd got a "persecution mania" – meaning she thought everyone was against her. But I've often wondered if what she said was true. And there's no way of knowing how the patients at the Grange are really treated.'

Bobby listened to all this with great interest and then said he was going for a walk before going to bed.

The Grange was, he knew, on the other side of the village from Merroway Court, so he turned in that direction. A lot of what he had heard could, of course, be explained. If Nicholson ran a place for curing drug takers, there *would* be strange sounds coming from it – but all the same, the story of the escaping girl worried Bobby.

At this point in his thoughts, Bobby arrived at a high wall with an entrance of metal gates, which were locked. He moved farther along the road, measuring the wall with his eye. Would it be possible to climb over? Suddenly he came across a little door. To his surprise *it* was not locked.

Bit of a mistake here, thought Bobby with a grin. He slipped through and found himself on a path, which twisted through bushes. Without warning, at a sharp turn, the path ended when it came to an open space close to the house and Bobby stepped full into the moonlight before he could stop himself.

At that moment a woman came round the corner of the house. She was walking very softly, glancing from side to side with – or so it seemed to Bobby – the fear of someone being hunted. Suddenly she stopped completely still and stood, moving from side to side as though she would fall. Bobby rushed forward and caught her. Her lips were white. He had never seen such awful fear on any human face before.

'It's all right,' he said reassuringly in a very low voice.

The girl moaned faintly, her eyelids half closed. 'I'm so frightened,' she whispered. 'I'm so terribly frightened.'

'What's the matter?' said Bobby.

Suddenly she seemed to hear something. She moved quickly away from Bobby. 'Go away!' she said.

'I want to help you,' said Bobby.

'Do you?' She looked at him, a strange, searching look. Then she shook her head. 'No one can help me.'

'I can,' said Bobby. 'Tell me what it is that frightens you so.'

She shook her head. 'Not now. Oh! Quick – they're coming! You can't help me unless you go now. At once – at once.'

Bobby gave in to her urgency. With a whispered, 'I'm at the *Anglers' Arms*,' he ran back along the path. Suddenly he heard footsteps on the path in front of him. Bobby stepped back quickly into the bushes just before a man passed – but it was too dark to see his face.

When he was sure the man was far enough away, Bobby got onto the path again, still trying to get over his shock at meeting the frightened girl. For he had recognized her beyond any possible doubt. *She* was the young woman in the photograph which had so mysteriously disappeared.

Chapter 16 Bobby Becomes a Lawyer

'It's extremely annoying,' Frankie said, 'to have to go up to London today. But the letter that Hawkins brought from Father yesterday says I must.'

'But,' said Roger, who had come out to say goodbye to her as she left Merroway Court, 'you'll be coming back this evening, won't you?'

He took her hand and held it between his hands. 'You *are* coming back?' he said with strange firmness.

Frankie laughed. 'Of course I am!'

Bobby, who was holding the car door open for her to get into the front passenger seat, touched his cap respectfully, then got in himself and drove off. 'Frankie,' he said, 'I've found the girl who was in the photograph I found in the dead man's pocket!'

'Oh, *Bobby*! Where?'

'In Dr Nicholson's nursing home.'

Bobby described what had happened the night before.

'Then we *are* on the right track,' Frankie said. 'And Dr Nicholson *is* mixed up in all this. I'm afraid of that man.'

'What's he like?'

'Oh, big, and he has a powerful personality – and he watched me so closely that I felt he knew the truth about me.'

She described the dinner party and Dr Nicholson's questions about her 'accident'. 'I think he was suspicious,' she finished.

'It's certainly strange that he went into details like that. But have you any idea now what's going on, Frankie?'

'Well, I think that Dr Nicholson's nursing home would be a very good cover up for illegal drug dealing. He might be pretending to cure drug addicts when he's really supplying them with the stuff.'

'That's possible,' agreed Bobby.

'And I haven't told you yet about Henry Bassington-ffrench!' said Frankie.

Bobby listened to her description of Henry's strange behaviour. 'And what about Roger Bassington-ffrench?' he asked.

'There I'm puzzled,' said Frankie. 'I have a strange feeling that he's innocent.'

'No,' said Bobby. 'He can't be. No one else could have exchanged the photographs.'

'I know,' said Frankie. 'But perhaps there's an innocent explanation.'

'I don't see that there can be. If we only had some idea who the dead man really was . . .'

'Oh, but I have, Bobby! I'm almost sure he was a man called Alan Carstairs.' Once more she told him everything she'd found out.

'You know,' said Bobby, 'we really are learning things. Now, we'll assume that you are right about Alan Carstairs. From what you say, he's lived abroad most of his adult life. He had very few friends in England, and if he disappeared, he wasn't likely to be missed. So, Carstairs comes down to Staverley with the Rivingtons. Now, did he get them to bring him deliberately, or was it just chance? And did he then come across the girl by accident just as I did? But he must have known her or he wouldn't have had her photograph on him.'

'Or,' said Frankie thoughtfully, 'he was already on the track of Nicholson and his gang for some reason.'

'And used the Rivingtons to get to Staverly?'

'That's a possible theory,' said Frankie.

'Or he may have been on the track of the girl,' said Bobby. 'Maybe he knew her. She may have been kidnapped and he came to England to find her.'

'But if he had tracked her down to Staverley, why would he go off to Wales?' asked Frankie.

'Obviously, there's a lot we don't know yet,' said Bobby.

'Evans, for example,' said Frankie thoughtfully. 'We don't have any clues yet about Evans. So that part of it *must* be connected with Wales.'

Frankie suddenly realised where they were. 'Bobby, we've reached London. Where are we going and what are we doing here?'

'That's for you to say,' said Bobby. 'I don't even know why we've come up to town.'

'The journey to London was only an excuse so that I could talk with you privately. I couldn't risk being seen walking about at Staverley talking to my chauffeur. I used the letter that we pretended had come from Father as an excuse for driving up to town. Well, I think we'd better go to my house in Brook Street. Your garage may be watched.'

Bobby, who lived in some rooms over the garage, agreed. At Brook Street they went upstairs to the big drawing-room.

'There's one other thing,' said Frankie. 'On the day you were poisoned, Roger Bassington-ffrench was at Staverley, but according to him, Nicholson was away at a conference in London.'

'And he has access to morphia,' said Bobby. 'It fits in nicely.'

Frankie picked up a telephone directory.

'What are you going to do?' Bobby asked.

'I'm looking up the name Rivington. There's a few of them but I think the Colonel Rivington who lives in Onslow Square or Mr R Rivington in Tite Street are the most likely ones. The Rivingtons, Bobby, have got to be seen immediately.'

'But what are we going to say?'

Frankie thought, then said, 'Do you feel you could be a lawyer?'

'But lawyers never make personal visits, do they? Surely they write and ask someone to come and see them at their office.'

'This firm does things differently,' said Frankie. She left the room and returned with a card. '*Mr Frederick Spragge*,' she said, handing it to Bobby. 'You are a member of the firm of Spragge, Spragge, Jenkinson and Spragge. They're Father's lawyers. The only Spragge left there is about a hundred, and he adores me. I'll fix things with him if the Rivingtons discover you're not a solicitor.'

'What about clothes? I can't go in my chauffeur's uniform.'

'We'd better attack Father's wardrobe.'

A quarter of an hour later, Bobby stood looking at himself in Lord Marchington's mirror.

'With these expensive clothes on me, I feel much more confident! Now, then, Frankie, do you think your father could lend me a hat?'

Chapter 17 Mrs Rivington Talks

Colonel Rivington was out. Mrs Rivington, however, was at home. Bobby was shown into a beautifully and expensively furnished drawing-room and shook hands with Mrs Rivington, who was beautifully and expensively dressed.

'I must apologize for coming to see you without warning, Mrs Rivington,' said Bobby. 'But the matter is urgent. It's about our client, Mr Alan Carstairs,' he said. 'He may have mentioned that we were working for him.'

'I believe he did,' said Mrs Rivington. She was clearly the type of woman who would agree to something rather than admit she didn't know about it, a woman with more beauty than brains.

'About Mr Carstairs . . .' said Bobby.

'We haven't seen him for some time. About . . . a month?'

'When you took him down to Staverley?'

'Yes. He'd just arrived in London and we were going down to Merroway Court for lunch, and up to Scotland next day for a couple of weeks, and Hubert really wanted to see Carstairs because he likes him so much, and so I said, "My dear, let's take him down to the Bassington-ffrenches with us. They won't mind." And we did. And, of course, they didn't mind.' She came breathlessly to a pause.

'Did he tell you his reasons for being in England?' asked Bobby.

'Oh, it was because of that millionaire, Savage, who was a friend of his. Savage's doctor told him he had cancer and he killed himself. So sad . . .'

'And did Mr Carstairs know the Bassington-ffrenches?'

'Oh, no! But I think he liked them. Though he was very quiet on the way back to London. I think something had upset him.'

'You don't know what it was? Did he meet any of the neighbours, perhaps?'

'No – unless he did so when he went out for a walk after lunch. But he did ask a lot of questions about some people who lived near the Bassington-ffrenches. Some doctor . . .'

'Dr Nicholson?'

'Yes. Alan wanted to know all about him and his wife. It seemed strange when he didn't know them. But what is it you wanted to know about Mr Carstairs?'

'I really wanted his address,' said Bobby. 'We've just had an important telegram from New York and need his instructions – but he hasn't left an address. And having heard him talk about you, I thought you might have news of him.'

'Oh, I see,' said Mrs Rivington. 'Well, I am very sorry but I have no idea where he's staying now.'

'I do apologize for taking up so much of your time,' said Bobby, getting up.

★ ★ ★

Back in Brook Street he and Frankie talked about what they had now learnt.

'It looks as though chance took Carstairs to the Bassington-ffrenches,' said Frankie. 'So it's *Nicholson* who is at the heart of the mystery.'

'Do you still insist that Roger Bassington-ffrench is innocent?' Bobby asked coldly.

'I can't believe he is a criminal.'

'You can't deny the evidence that he changed the photograph.'

'Damn the photograph!' said Frankie.

Bobby drove up to Merroway Court in silence. Frankie got out of the car and went into the house without looking back. She opened the door of the library – and stopped. Dr Nicholson was sitting on the sofa, holding Sylvia Bassington-ffrench's hands.

Sylvia jumped to her feet and came across to Frankie.

'He's been telling me about Henry's drug addiction.' She was crying. 'It's terrible!' And she ran out of the room.

Dr Nicholson had got up. His eyes, watchful as always, met Frankie's. 'Poor lady,' he said. 'It has been a great shock. But it is best that she knows the truth. I want her to persuade her husband to become a patient at my nursing home.'

Chapter 18 The Girl of the Photograph

On Bobby's return to the *Angler's Arms* he was told that someone was waiting to see him.

'It's a lady. You'll find her in the little sitting-room.'

Wondering who it could be, Bobby went into the room. Sitting on a chair was a slim figure dressed in black – the girl of the photograph. Her hands were shaking and her large eyes held a terrified question.

'You said – you said – you'd help me . . .'

'Of course I'll help you,' Bobby said. 'Don't be frightened. You're quite safe now.'

'Who are you?' she asked. 'You're – you're – not really a chauffeur, are you?'

'No – but that doesn't matter now. Trust me – and tell me all about it.'

'You must think I'm completely mad.'

'No, no.'

'Yes – coming here like this. But I was so frightened . . .'

Bobby took her hand firmly. 'Look here, everything's going to be all right. You're safe now.'

'When you stepped out into the moonlight the other night,' she said, 'it was like a dream, and I decided later that I would come and find you, and – tell you everything. But – but you'll think I've gone mad from being in that place with those truly mad people.'

'No, I won't. Please, tell me . . .'

She stared straight in front of her. 'I'm afraid I'm going to be murdered.'

'Murdered?' Bobby exclaimed. 'Who wants to murder you?'

'My husband . . .'

'Your husband? Who are you?' he asked. 'And who is your husband?'

It was her turn to look surprised. 'Don't you know? I'm Moira Nicholson. My husband is Dr Nicholson!'

'And you . . . you're telling me your husband wants to murder you?'

'Yes. Strange things have happened to me – accidents!'

'Accidents?' said Bobby sharply.

'Yes. Oh! I know it sounds mad, but he reversed the car, not seeing I was there, he said later – I managed to jump aside – and there were some pills that were in the wrong bottle. It's exhausting me watching out for myself all the time – trying to save my life.'

'Why does your husband want to kill you?' asked Bobby.

'Because he wants to marry Sylvia Bassington-ffrench. He's trying to get Mr Bassington-ffrench to come to the Grange as a patient. Then something would happen to him there, I'm sure.' She shivered. 'He's got some power over Mr Bassington-ffrench but I don't know what it is.'

'Bassington-ffrench takes morphia,' said Bobby.

'Is that it? Jasper gives it to him, I suppose.'

'It comes by post.'

'Jasper's as cunning as a fox. If he posts the drugs to Henry Bassington-ffrench, no one will know they're from him.' She shivered. 'All sorts of things happen at the Grange. People come there to get better – and they don't – they get worse.'

Bobby said, 'You say your husband wants to marry Mrs Bassington-ffrench?'

Moira nodded. 'He's crazy about her.'

'And she?'

'I don't know,' said Moira slowly. 'She seems to be a simple woman, fond of her husband and little boy. But sometimes I've wondered if she is an entirely different woman from the one we all think she is . . . if she isn't playing a part . . .'

'What about the brother, Roger?' asked Bobby.

'I don't know much about him. He's nice, I think, but he's completely fooled by Jasper.'

Bobby was silent a minute or two, trying to decide what to do. 'Look here,' he said. 'I'm going to ask you a question straight out. Did you know a man called Alan Carstairs and at some time give him your photograph?'

He saw her cheeks go red. 'Yes.'

'Has he been down here to see you since you were married?'

'Yes. I don't know how he knew I was living here. I had never written to him since my marriage.'

'But he found out and came. About a month ago?'

'Yes.'

'Did you tell Carstairs your fears about your husband and the nursing home?'

She shook her head. 'I tried not to show in any way that my marriage hadn't been a success.'

'But he might have guessed it all the same,' said Bobby gently.

'I suppose he might,' she admitted in a low voice.

'Do you think that he knew anything about your husband – that he suspected, for instance, that this nursing home place mightn't be quite what it seemed to be?'

'It's possible,' she said at last. 'He asked one or two strange questions – but, no, I don't think he can really have known anything about it.'

Bobby was silent again for a few minutes. Then he said, 'Would you call your husband a jealous man? Jealous, for instance, about you.'

'Yes. Very. He thinks he owns me, you see.' She shivered again. Then she asked suddenly, 'You're not connected with the police, are you?'

'I? Oh, no!'

'I wondered, I mean . . .'

Bobby looked down at his chauffeur's uniform. 'It's a long story.'

'You are Lady Frances Derwent's chauffeur, aren't you? So the owner of the pub here said. I met her at dinner the other night.'

'I know.' He paused. 'We've got to have a conversation with Frankie to discuss things. Do you think you could ring up and get her to meet you somewhere? I know it must seem really strange to you that I can't do it. But it won't be when I've explained.'

Moira stood. 'Very well.' At the door she stopped. 'Alan,' she said, 'Alan Carstairs. Did you say you'd seen him?'

And, Bobby thought, shocked, she doesn't know he's dead. He said, 'Ring up Lady Frances. Then I'll tell you everything.'

Chapter 19 A Meeting of Three

Moira came back a few minutes later. 'I've asked her to meet me at a place where we can sit near the river,' she said.

While they waited for Frankie, Bobby felt he must try and explain everything that had happened. 'There's a lot to tell you,' he said. 'To begin with, I'm not a chauffeur. And my name isn't Hawkins – it's Jones – Bobby Jones. I come from Marchbolt in Wales.'

Clearly, Marchbolt meant nothing to her. Bobby went bravely to the terrible news he had to tell her. 'I'm afraid I'm going to give you rather a shock. This friend of yours – Alan Carstairs, he's – he's dead.'

To his surprise, she looked sad – but that was all.

'He fell over the cliff at Marchbolt,' Bobby said. 'He had your photograph in his pocket.'

'Did he?' She gave a sweet, sad smile. 'Dear Alan, he was – very loyal.'

'Did he tell you he was going to Wales?'

She shook her head.

'You don't know anyone called Evans, do you?' said Bobby.

'Evans? No. It's a very common name, of course, but I can't remember anybody. What is he?'

'That's just what we don't know. Oh, here's Frankie.'

Frankie came hurrying along the path.

'Hello, Frankie,' said Bobby. 'We've got to have a serious talk. To begin with, it's Mrs Nicholson who is the original of *the* photograph.'

'Oh!' said Frankie. She looked at Moira and suddenly laughed.

'My dear,' she said to Bobby, 'now I see why the sight of Mrs Cayman was such a shock to you!'

'Exactly,' said Bobby.

Moira was looking confused.

'Let me explain,' Frankie said. She went straight into the story. But, once she had explained their conclusion that Bassington-ffrench must have pushed Carstairs over the cliff, she was brought to a stop by the look on Moira's face.

'Roger Bassington-ffrench?' Moira's voice was amused.

'Your photograph disappeared – and only he could have taken it.'

'I see,' said Moira thoughtfully.

'Facts are facts,' said Bobby.

'No.' Moira shook her head. 'Roger might be weak – or wild. But pushing someone over a cliff – no, I can't imagine it.'

'But he must have taken that photograph,' said Bobby.

'Yes. It seems very strange.' Moira paused for a moment and then said unexpectedly, 'Why don't you ask him?'

Chapter 20 Meeting of Two

For a moment, the simplicity of the question took their breath away.

'You see,' said Moira, 'Roger *must* have taken that photograph, but I don't believe he pushed Alan over. Why should he? They had only met once – at lunch down here. There's no motive.'

'Then who *did* push him over?' asked Frankie directly.

'Moira,' said Bobby. 'Do you mind if I tell Frankie what you're afraid of?'

Moira turned her head away. 'If you like. But I can't believe it myself at this minute. I feel I've been terribly silly. Please don't pay any attention to what I said, Mr Jones. It was just – nerves. I must go now. Goodbye.'

Bobby jumped up to follow her, but Frankie pushed him back. 'Stay there, leave this to me.' She went quickly off after Moira. She returned a few minutes later.

'Well?' asked Bobby anxiously.

'I calmed her down and made her promise we'd meet again soon. Now tell me everything.'

Bobby did so, then Frankie said, 'It fits in with what I've just seen. I found Nicholson holding Sylvia Bassington-ffrench's hands – and if the look he gave me could kill, I'd have been dead then and there. But why would Nicholson want to get rid of Alan Carstairs?'

'A large coincidence if Carstairs and Bassington-ffrench were in Marchbolt on the same day.'

'Well, coincidences do happen. But I don't see the motive. Was Carstairs on the track of Nicholson as the head of a drug-dealing gang? Or is Moira the motive for the murder?'

'It might be both,' suggested Bobby. 'Nicholson might have known that Carstairs and Moira had talked and he may have believed that his wife had betrayed his secrets.'

'That's a possibility,' said Frankie. 'Now, the first thing to do is to talk to Roger Bassington-ffrench. If he can clear up the exchange of the photographs, it might be very valuable to have him on our side.'

'How do you mean, Frankie?'

'Bobby, if Moira's husband wants to get rid of her and marry Sylvia, then Henry Bassington-ffrench is in serious danger, too. We've got to prevent him being sent to the Grange. And at present Roger Bassington-ffrench is on Nicholson's side.'

'Well thought of, Frankie,' said Bobby quietly. 'Go ahead with your plan.'

Frankie got up to go. 'Isn't it odd?' she said. 'We seem, somehow, to have got in between the covers of a book. We're in the middle of someone else's story. It's a very strange feeling.'

'I know what you mean,' said Bobby. 'But I would call it a play rather than a book. It's as though we'd walked on to the stage in the middle of the play and we haven't the slightest idea what the beginning was about. And what brought us into the show was a regular cue – five words – which are quite meaningless as far as we are concerned.'

'"*Why didn't they ask Evans?*" Isn't it odd, Bobby, that though we've found out a lot, and more characters have come into the thing, we never get any nearer to the mysterious Evans? Sometimes, I don't believe there is an Evans.'

Saying that, she went back towards the house.

Chapter 21 Roger Answers a Question

Frankie found Roger in the garden. 'There's something I want to ask you,' she said immediately. 'Do you mind telling me if you took a photograph out of that man's pocket – at Marchbolt?'

She saw a look of slight annoyance on his face – but no guilt or worry.

'Now, how on earth did you guess that?'

'You *did* take it! Why?'

Roger seemed embarrassed. 'Well, look at it as I did. Here I am, looking after a dead body. Something is sticking out of his pocket. The photograph of a woman I know – a married woman. What's going to happen? An inquest. Publicity. Possibly the poor girl's name in all the newspapers. I acted without thinking. Took the photo and tore it up. I didn't want Moira to get into trouble.'

Frankie took in a deep breath. 'But you should have told the police the man was Alan Carstairs. You must have recognized him!'

'I never saw his face! There was a handkerchief over it.'

'You never thought of looking?' asked Frankie.

'No. Why should I?'

How typical of a man! thought Frankie. A woman would certainly have looked. Then, aloud, she said, 'Sit down, I'm going to tell you a lot of things . . .'

'I think you must be right,' he said when she had finished. 'Alan Carstairs *was* murdered. But I don't see why you see Nicholson as the criminal.'

'There are all the things Mrs Nicholson told Bobby.'

Roger frowned. 'She may honestly believe he is trying to kill her – but is it true? She thinks he supplies Henry with the drug – but she has no evidence. She thinks he's in love with Sylvia. Well – lots of respectable men fall in love with other people's wives. No. It seems to me you're ignoring the real suspects. The Caymans.'

'So you think Carstairs was carrying a photograph of Mrs Cayman as well as Mrs Nicholson's?'

Roger nodded. 'I think one was love and the other was business!'

'You're right,' Frankie agreed. 'We ought to track the Caymans. But what about your brother. Do you still think he should go to the Grange?'

'No,' said Roger. 'I don't. I think I'll ring up Nicholson. I'd like to have a talk with him.'

He went quickly into the house as an aeroplane passed low overhead, filling the air with the sound of its loud engines. It disappeared over the trees, its noise lessening, and soon Roger came out again. He seemed slightly breathless. 'Nicholson isn't in,' he said. 'I left a message.'

They sat down on the garden seat and Roger agreed with Frankie that to tell the whole story to Sylvia would be a mistake. The best plan would be to question the doctor.

'Henry mustn't go to the Grange,' Roger said. 'You know – what's that?' They both jumped up.

'It sounded like a shot,' said Frankie. They ran towards the house and went in by the glass doors of the drawing-room.

Sylvia was in the hall, her face white as paper. 'Did you hear?' she said. 'It was a shot – from Henry's study.'

Roger put an arm round her. Frankie went to the study door and turned the handle. 'It's locked,' she said.

'The window,' said Roger. He ran out again through the drawing-room, Frankie at his heels. They ran round the house till they came to the study window. It was closed, and they could see Henry Bassington-ffrench lying across his desk. There was a bullet wound in his forehead and a gun lay on the floor.

'He's shot himself,' said Frankie.

'Stand back,' said Roger. 'I'm going to break the window.' He took off his jacket and wrapped it round his hand then smashed the glass. He and Frankie stepped into the room. As they did so, Sylvia and Dr Nicholson came hurrying along the terrace.

'Here's the doctor,' said Sylvia. 'He's just arrived. I saw him coming up the drive.'

Then she saw her husband and cried out. Roger stepped quickly out through the window and Dr Nicholson pushed Sylvia into his arms.

'Take her away,' he said. 'Look after her.' He stepped through the window and joined Frankie. 'This is a terrible business,' he said. 'Poor fellow. He must have felt he couldn't give up his drugs. Too bad. Too bad. I wonder if he wrote something first. They usually do.'

Frankie looked down at the desk. A piece of paper, with a few words written on it, lay at Bassington-ffrench's elbow.

I feel this is the best way out. This dreadful habit has taken too great a hold on me for me to fight it now. I want to do the best I can for Sylvia and Tommy. God bless you both, my dears. Forgive me …

Frankie felt suddenly sick.

Chapter 22 Moira Disappears

Frankie rang Bobby an hour later and told him the news.

'We must meet. I'll go for a walk before breakfast. Say eight o'clock – the same place we met today.'

Bobby arrived first, but Frankie did not keep him waiting long. She looked pale and upset. 'Hello, Bobby, it's so terrible. I haven't been able to sleep all night. I will have to leave today, of course. Sylvia's collapsed, poor woman.'

Bobby nodded. 'Is it quite certain that he did commit suicide? Moira said that Nicholson wanted two people out of the way – and *here's one of them gone.*'

'It *must* be suicide,' Frankie said, 'the study door was locked and so was the window – Roger had to smash it. It was only then that Nicholson appeared. Honestly, Bobby, Nicholson could not have killed Henry. Sylvia was in the house when the shot was fired and she actually saw Nicholson coming up the drive. I hate to say it, but the man has an alibi.'

'I distrust people who have alibis,' said Bobby. 'Well, what do we investigate next?'

'The Caymans. Do you agree?'

'Absolutely. And if Moira's right and Nicholson wants to marry Sylvia, Moira's life is in great danger. We must persuade her to leave the Grange at once!'

Frankie nodded. 'Bring the car round at half-past ten. We'll drive straight to the Grange.'

* * *

Frankie had never been to the Grange before and the big iron gates and large dark green bushes depressed her. 'It's a scary place,' she observed.

They drove up to the front door and Bobby got out of the car and rang the bell. A nurse opened the door.

'Mrs Nicholson?' said Bobby.

The woman opened the door wider. Frankie got out of the car and went into the house. She followed the nurse upstairs, into the small sitting-room decorated with bright curtains and many vases of flowers. The nurse went out and five minutes later Dr Nicholson came in.

Frankie hid the worry she felt with a welcoming smile and shook his hand.

'Good morning, Lady Frances. You've not come to bring me bad news of Mrs Bassington-ffrench, I hope?'

'She was still asleep when I left,' said Frankie. 'I really called to see your wife.'

'That was very kind of you.'

Was it only her imagination, or did the pale-blue eyes show dislike?

'I want to ask her to come to me in Marchbolt for a visit.' Frankie smiled again.

'Why, that's really very kind of you, Lady Frances. I'm sure Moira would have enjoyed that very much.'

'Would have?' asked Frankie sharply.

Dr Nicholson smiled. 'Unfortunately, my wife went away this morning. This is rather a sad place for a young woman, Lady Frances. Occasionally Moira feels she must have a little excitement.'

'You don't know where she has gone?'

'London, I imagine. Shoes and theatres. You know the sort of thing.'

Frankie felt that his smile was the most unpleasant thing she had ever seen.

Chapter 23 On the Track of the Caymans

Bobby had to work hard to keep his face from showing his feelings when he saw Frankie come out alone. He drove down the drive and out through the gates. Then he stopped the car. 'What's going on?' he asked.

Rather pale, Frankie replied, 'Bobby, I don't like it. Nicholson says she's gone away.'

'We should never have let her go back there yesterday.'

'You don't think she's – dead, do you?' whispered Frankie in a shaky voice.

'No.' said Bobby. 'Her death would have to seem natural and accidental. No, I believe she's still at the Grange.'

'Well,' said Frankie, 'what are we going to do?'

Bobby thought for a minute. 'You'd better go back to London and go on with tracing the Caymans. I'll drive you and then your chauffeur will disappear. I'll remove my moustache then come back down here and get a room at Ambledever – that's only ten miles away but it's unlikely that Roger will see me there and recognise me from Marchbolt – and if Moira's still in the Grange, I'll find her.'

'Bobby, you *will* be careful?'

'I will be – I promise, Frankie.'

* * *

At three o'clock that afternoon Frankie arrived at St Leonard's Gardens, Paddington. She stopped at number 17 where there were no Caymans and a sign outside said that it was available to be rented.

Frankie wrote down the house agent's address and set off. But the Caymans had left no forwarding address with the agent. Disappointed, Frankie bought a newspaper and read it on the Tube to Piccadilly Circus. There was a paragraph about Sir John Milkington recovering after his accident aboard the *Astradora,* the famous yacht which had belonged to the late Mr John Savage, the millionaire. Was it an unlucky boat? asked the writer.

Frankie frowned. Twice before she'd heard the name of John Savage – from Sylvia Bassington-ffrench when she was speaking of Alan Carstairs, and from Bobby when he was repeating the conversation he had had with Mrs Rivington. Alan Carstairs had been a friend of John Savage's. And Savage had committed suicide because he thought he had cancer.

Supposing Alan Carstairs had not been satisfied with the story of his friend's death. What if he had come over to investigate that death? Perhaps it was *Savage's* death that was the beginning of the play that she and Bobby were acting in.

'It's possible,' thought Frankie.

She had no idea who John Savage's friends had been – then an idea came to her – his will! If there had been something suspicious about his death, his will might give her a clue.

* * *

Frankie was received with a great deal of respect at *Spragge, Spragge, Jenkinson & Spragge* and was shown into the private office of Mr Spragge, the senior member of the firm, who, it was said, knew more dark secrets about aristocratic families than any other man in London.

'Lady Frances,' said Mr Spragge. 'Do sit down. And what is it that gives me the pleasure of seeing you this afternoon?'

'I want to look at a will,' said Frankie. 'And I don't know where to go to see it.'

'You go to *Somerset House.* All wills are stored there,' said Mr Spragge. 'But I can tell you anything you want to know about the wills in your family.'

'It isn't a family will,' said Frankie. 'I wanted to see the will of Mr John Savage.'

'Indeed?' Mr Spragge looked worried. 'Lady Frances, I would never want to involve you in anything that might be illegal, and there is something going on that worries me. I have been impersonated, Lady Frances. Deliberately impersonated. What do you say to that?'

For a moment Frankie, suddenly in a panic, could say nothing at all. Then, 'How did you find out?' she asked.

'Do you know something about this impersonation, Lady Frances?'

Frankie said weakly, 'It was a joke . . .'

'And who,' demanded Mr Spragge, 'pretended to be me?'

Knowing his weakness for aristocratic names, Frankie said, 'It was the young Duke of – no, I really *mustn't* mention names.'

Mr Spragge's kind manner returned. 'Oh, you young people!' he said, smiling, and putting a letter into her hand, 'There, see where your foolishness has led you into.'

> *Dear Mr Spragge,* (Mrs Rivington had written), *I've just remembered something that might have helped you the day you called on me. Alan Carstairs mentioned that he was going to a place called Chipping Somerton. With kind regards,*
>
> *Edith Rivington.*

'I understood that there was some extremely questionable business,' said Mr Spragge, 'with my client, Mr Carstairs . . .'

'Was Alan Carstairs a client of yours?' Frankie interrupted excitedly.

'He was. He came to me for advice when he was last in England.'

'He came to ask you about Mr Savage's will, didn't he?' said Frankie.

'Ah! It was *you* who advised him to come to me?'

'Would it be unprofessional of you to tell me your advice?' she asked, avoiding answering the question.

'Not in this case,' said Mr Spragge. 'My opinion was that there was nothing that could be done.'

'The whole thing was very strange,' said Frankie, pushing gently. She felt as if she was walking barefoot over a floor covered with broken glass. At any minute she might step on a bit . . .

'Such cases are less uncommon than you might think,' said Mr Spragge.

'Cases of suicide?'

'No, cases of men being persuaded to do things they wouldn't usually do by a pretty girl. Mr Savage was a hard-headed businessman – and yet he seems to have fallen completely under this woman's influence.'

'I wish you'd tell me the whole story,' said Frankie. 'Mr Carstairs was so angry when he spoke of it that I never understood it clearly.'

'Mr Savage was extremely wealthy. On a voyage back from the United States he met a Mrs Templeton.' Mr Spragge shook his head sadly. 'Mr Savage was very much attracted to her. He accepted the lady's invitation to stay at her cottage at Chipping Somerton, where he came more and more under her spell. Then came the tragedy. Mr Savage had, for some time, been uneasy about his health. He feared he might be suffering from cancer. It became an obsession. The Templetons persuaded him to go up to London and see a specialist. He did so. Now, Lady Frances, that specialist – a highly respected doctor – swore at the inquest that Mr Savage was *not* suffering from cancer, but that Mr Savage was so obsessed by his own belief that he could not accept the truth when he was told it.

'Anyway, Mr Savage went back to Chipping Somerton in a state of great sadness. He saw ahead of him a painful and slow death – and he was determined not to go through it. He sent for a lawyer and made a will, which he signed. That same evening Mr Savage took a very large dose of a sleeping drug, leaving a letter in which he said he preferred a quick and painless death to a long and painful one. And by his will, Mr Savage left seven hundred thousand pounds to Mrs Templeton and the rest to charities.'

Mr Spragge leaned back in his chair. 'The jury brought in the verdict of Suicide while of Unsound Mind. But the will was made in the presence of a lawyer who believed that Savage *was* of sound mind.' Mr Spragge paused. 'Mr Carstairs, however, believed that such a will was completely against Mr Savage's beliefs. He disliked organized charities and held very strong opinions that money should be left to blood relatives. However, Mr Carstairs had no written proof of these beliefs – and Mr Savage's only relatives were distant cousins in Australia without the money to challenge the will.'

'I see,' said Frankie. 'Is anything known about this Mrs Templeton?'

Mr Spragge shook his head. 'Nothing, except that she was very beautiful. A man like Mr Savage ought not to have been deceived – but . . .' Mr Spragge shook his head as the faces of many clients who ought to have known better passed across his mind.

Frankie rose. 'Men are extraordinary creatures,' she said.

Chapter 24 'My Brother was Murdered'

On Friday morning Frankie's car stopped outside the Station Hotel at Ambledever. She had sent a telegram to Bobby telling him that she would have to attend the inquest on Henry Bassington-ffrench and would stop and see him on the way down from London. She had expected a telegram in reply – but nothing had come.

'Yes, Miss,' said the hotel receptionist. 'Mr Jones came here on Wednesday evening. He left his bag and said he mightn't be in till late. He hasn't been back.'

Frankie felt sick. 'Did he leave any message?'

The man shook his head. 'Anything I can do, Miss?'

Frankie shook her head. She must have time to think about what to do next.

The inquest took place at Merroway Court. Roger was there and Sylvia – looking very beautiful in her black suit. The verdict was 'Suicide while of Unsound Mind', just as the verdict in John Savage's death had been.

Two suicides while of Unsound Mind, thought Frankie. Could there be a connection?

Frankie and Dr Nicholson stayed behind after everyone else left.

'I think there are some letters for you, Frankie, dear,' said Sylvia. 'You won't mind if I leave you and go and lie down, will you? It's been so awful.'

She shivered and left the room.

'That went very well,' Dr Nicholson said. 'We are lucky that Dr Davidson was our coroner.'

'I suppose so,' said Frankie.

'It makes a lot of difference, Lady Frances. The coroner can make things as easy or as difficult as he pleases. In this case everything went perfectly.'

'A good stage performance, in fact,' said Frankie in a hard voice.

Nicholson looked at her in surprise.

'I know what Lady Frances is thinking,' said Roger. 'My brother was *murdered*, Dr Nicholson. The criminals who made my brother a slave to drugs murdered him – just as if they had shot him.'

Roger's angry eyes looked straight into the doctor's. 'Somehow, I mean to make them pay for that.'

Dr Nicholson shook his head sadly. 'I agree with you, Mr Bassington-ffrench. It is a terrible crime to persuade a man to take drugs.' He turned to Frankie. 'You came down by car, Lady Frances? No accidents this time?'

'No,' she said. 'I think it's a pity to have too many accidents – don't you?'

His eyebrows rose. 'Perhaps your chauffeur drove you this time?'

'My chauffeur,' said Frankie, 'has disappeared. He was last known to be heading for the Grange.'

'Really?' Nicholson's voice sounded amused. 'I can't believe it. Possibly you are paying too much attention to local gossip. It is very unreliable. I even heard a story that my wife and your chauffeur had been seen talking together down by the river, Lady Frances.'

Is that his plan? thought Frankie. Is he going to pretend that his wife has gone away with my chauffeur?

Nicholson turned to Roger. 'I must be going. Believe me, all my sympathies are with you and Mrs Bassington-ffrench.'

Roger went out into the hall with him. Frankie followed. On the hall table were a couple of letters addressed to her. One was from her father. The other . . . The other was in Bobby's handwriting! She tore it open.

Dear Frankie,

Follow me as soon as possible to Chipping Somerton. Come by train. The Bentley is too noticeable. Come to a house called Tudor Cottage – I've put instructions on how to get there below. Don't tell anyone at all.

Yours ever,
Bobby

Nothing terrible had happened to Bobby. And he was going to the place she had intended them to go to together! Because she had been to *Somerset House* to look up the will of John Savage and in it, Mrs Templeton – Rose Templeton – was said to be the wife of Edgar Templeton of Tudor Cottage, Chipping Somerton. They were reaching the end of the play.

★ ★ ★

It was getting dark and just beginning to rain when Frankie's train arrived at the little station of Chipping Somerton. Frankie buttoned her coat to her neck and set off. She saw the lights of the village ahead and, following the instructions Bobby had sent, turned left onto a narrow road that went uphill. At the top she took the right-hand path and soon saw the pine trees Bobby had described. Finally she came to a gate and, lighting a match, saw Tudor Cottage written on it. Her heart began beating a little faster when she saw the door open and a figure in chauffeur's uniform look cautiously out. Bobby! He waved his hand for her to come then went back inside.

Frankie came up to the door. Everything was dark and silent.

'Bobby?' she whispered as she stepped inside.

Strong arms grabbed her and a wet cloth was put over her mouth. The smell of chloroform filled her nose. She fought desperately, twisting and turning. Then everything went black . . .

Chapter 25 At the Eleventh Hour

When Frankie woke up she was lying on a hard wooden floor and her hands and feet were tied. She heard a human sound and looked about her. She seemed to be in the attic room at the top of the cottage. The only light came from a window in the roof – and there was little of that. In a few minutes it would be quite dark. There were a few broken pictures lying against the wall and some broken chairs. The sound had come from the corner. Frankie managed a sideways movement across the floor.

'Bobby!'

Bobby was also tied up. In addition, he had a cloth tied round his mouth, which he had almost succeeded in getting loose. Frankie helped him by pulling at the cloth with her teeth. When it came off, Bobby said, 'Frankie!'

'I'm glad we're together,' said Frankie. 'But it does look as though we've been idiots. Did they kidnap you after you wrote to me?'

'I never wrote,' Bobby said. 'I was hit on the head at the Grange and woke up here.'

Frankie told him her adventures. 'And then they chloroformed me,' she finished.

'We've got to get out of here, Frankie. Your wrists are more loosely tied than mine. Let's see if I can undo them with my teeth.'

Bobby spent the next five minutes struggling with the rope round Frankie's wrists.

Then she said, 'There's someone coming!' She rolled away from him. Heavy footsteps could be heard coming up the stairs. A key turned in the lock and the door opened.

'And how are my two little birds?' said the voice of Dr Nicholson. He carried a candle and was wearing a hat pulled down over his eyes, glasses, and a heavy overcoat with the collar turned up, so they couldn't see his face. He shook his head at them. 'I am surprised, my dear young lady, that you fell into the trap so easily. Let me see if you are comfortable.'

He examined Bobby's ropes and passed on to Frankie. He shook his head. 'Your young friend's teeth, I see, have been active.'

Nicholson picked up Frankie, sat her on a chair and tied her to it. 'Not too uncomfortable, I hope?' he said. 'Well, it isn't for long.'

'What are you going to do with us?' she demanded.

'You taunted me, Lady Frances, with being too fond of accidents. I am going to risk one more. Lady Frances Derwent, driving her car, her chauffeur beside her, takes a wrong turning. The car crashes over the edge of a cliff. Lady Frances and her chauffeur are killed.'

'He is enjoying this,' thought Bobby. 'Really enjoying it.'

Nicholson turned to the door.

'What about your wife?' cried Bobby. 'Have you murdered her, too?'

'Moira is still alive,' said Nicholson. 'How much longer she remains so depends on what happens in the next few hours.' He smiled unpleasantly. 'Goodbye for now. It will take me a couple of hours to complete my arrangements.' He went out and locked the door behind him.

'Frankie!' said Bobby. 'That wasn't Nicholson.'

'Have you gone mad?'

'It *wasn't* Nicholson, Frankie. At the Grange I watched through a window while Nicholson worked at his desk. I noticed that his ears were small and laid flat against his head. That man's ears weren't like that. This is a very clever actor impersonating Nicholson.'

'But why – and who?'

'*Roger Bassington-ffrench*,' said Bobby.

'Bassington-ffrench!' whispered Frankie. 'Bobby, you're right. He was the only person there when I taunted Nicholson about accidents.'

'He's been too clever for us, Frankie,' said Bobby. 'Moira's a prisoner; you and I are tied hand and foot. And nobody else has any idea where we are.'

The next minute, with a loud crash, a body fell through the roof window and from among a pile of broken glass, a voice spoke. 'Bobby!'

'Gosh!' said Bobby. 'It's Badger!'

Chapter 26 Badger's Story

There was not a minute to be lost. Already sounds could be heard on the floor below.

'Quick, Badger!' said Bobby. 'Pull one of my boots off! Put it down in the middle of the broken glass and crawl under that bed! Quick!'

Steps were coming up the stairs. The key turned. Bassington-ffrench stood in the doorway. He stared in amazement – from the broken window, to the boot, to Bobby's bootless left foot.

'I can hardly believe it, my young friend,' he said. 'Extremely acrobatic.'

He examined the ropes that bound Bobby – then looked at him curiously. 'I wish I knew how you managed that.' Then, shaking his head, he left the room.

Badger crawled out from under the bed. He had a small pocketknife and soon cut the other two free.

'That's better,' said Bobby, stretching his arms. 'Well, Frankie, what about our friend Nicholson?'

'You're right,' said Frankie. 'Now that I *know* he's Roger Bassington-ffrench I can see it. But it's a pretty good performance all the same.'

'I was at Oxford with a Bassington-ffrench,' said Badger. 'Marvellous actor. Bad man, though. He forged his father's name on a cheque.'

'Forgery,' said Frankie thoughtfully. 'That letter from you, Bobby, was really well done.'

'What are we going to do next?' Badger asked.

'We're going to go behind this door,' said Bobby. 'And when our friend returns, you and I are going to give him the surprise of his life. How about it, Badger? Are you ready?'

'Oh yes!'

'Now. How did you get here? And why did you fall through the window?'

'Well, you see,' said Badger, 'after you went off, I had some problems.'

The story was a typical Badger tale of having no money and of someone demanding that he paid a bill. Bobby had gone away, leaving no address, just saying that he was driving the Bentley down to Staverley. So to Staverley came Badger. 'I thought perhaps you might be able to let me have five pounds,' he explained.

Badger had come across the Bentley parked outside a pub – empty.

'So I thought I'd give you a surprise. There were some blankets on the back seat and there was nobody about. I got in and pulled them over me.'

A chauffeur had come out of the pub and Badger, looking out from his hiding place, was amazed to see that this was not Bobby. Badger did not know what to do next. Explanations and apologies to the driver would be difficult, so Badger decided to lie still and get himself out of the car without being seen when it stopped.

The car reached Tudor Cottage and the chauffeur drove it into the garage and left it there. There was a small window in the garage and through this Badger had seen Frankie arrive and go into the house.

When he realised that the there were no lights in the house, Badger began to suspect something was wrong. He decided to have a look round. The windows on the ground floor all had their curtains closed, but he thought that by getting on to the roof he might manage to have a look into the windows there.

He got up onto the garage roof and from there to the roof of the cottage. Then, when he had knelt down to look in the attic window, he'd slipped and fallen on the glass.

Bobby took in a long breath. 'If it wasn't for you, Badger, my friend, Frankie and I would have been murdered. It must have been Bassington-ffrench you saw, dressed up in my chauffeur's uniform and pretending to be me so that no one would realise I'd disappeared.'

He gave Badger a short explanation of what he and Frankie had been doing, then he said, 'Someone's coming!'

Badger and Bobby hid behind the door and, as Bassington-ffrench came into the room, they jumped on him. A few seconds later the three friends stood looking down with pleasure at a man who was securely tied up.

'Good evening, Mr Bassington-ffrench,' said Bobby. 'How nice to see you again!'

Chapter 27 Escape

The man on the floor spoke. 'Very interesting,' he said. 'I really knew that no man tied up as you were *could* have thrown a boot through that window. But because the boot was there among the broken glass, I assumed that, though it was impossible, the impossible had been achieved. So, this is most unexpected. I thought I'd got you all fooled nicely.'

'So you had,' said Frankie. 'You forged that letter from Bobby, I suppose?'

'I did,' said Roger, smiling.

'And the letter from Moira?' demanded Bobby.

Roger laughed. 'Forgery is a very useful art.'

'You pig!' said Bobby.

Frankie was curious. 'Why did you pretend to be Dr Nicholson?' she asked.

'For the fun of seeing whether I could fool you both. You were so very sure that poor old Nicholson was the evil criminal, Lady Frances.' He laughed. 'Just because he questioned you in his serious way.'

'And really,' said Frankie slowly, 'he was quite innocent? There's one thing you must tell me. I've been driven nearly mad with curiosity. Who is Evans?'

'Oh!' said Bassington-ffrench. 'So you don't know that?' He laughed – and laughed again. 'That shows what a fool one can be.'

'Meaning us?' asked Frankie.

'No,' said Roger. 'Meaning me. And if you don't know who Evans is, I don't think I will tell you.'

Somehow, even though Bassington-ffrench was tied up and a prisoner, it was he who seemed to control the situation. 'And what are your plans now?' he asked.

Bobby said something about the police.

'Much the best thing to do,' said Roger cheerfully. 'They will charge me with kidnap, I suppose. I can't very well deny that.' He looked at Frankie. 'I will use love as my excuse.'

Frankie's face reddened. 'What about murder of Alan Carstairs?' she asked.

'My dear, you haven't any evidence.'

'We'd better go downstairs together,' Bobby said. 'We don't know how many more of the gang are in the house. And we'd better look into the bedrooms first.'

Three bedrooms were empty. In the fourth, a slim figure was lying unconscious on the bed.

'It's Moira!' cried Frankie. 'She's drugged!' A syringe lay on a table near the window. 'We ought to get a doctor.'

The telephone was in the hall below. They got through to the police station and ten minutes later a car arrived with an inspector, a uniformed policeman and an elderly doctor.

Bobby led the way upstairs to the attic – then stood, extremely surprised, in the doorway. A chair had been placed on the bed, which had been dragged underneath the broken window. There was no sign of Roger Bassington-ffrench.

Chapter 28 Frankie Asks a Question

Exhausted by her adventures, Frankie slept late the next morning. It was half-past ten when she came down to the lounge of the *Station Hotel* to find Bobby waiting for her. 'Hello, Frankie, here you are at last.'

'Don't be so horribly energetic! What is the matter with you?'

'I feel absolutely *full* of energy,' said Bobby. 'I've been with Inspector Hammond for the last half-hour and he seems to think we've been playing some kind of joke. So *we've* got to find out exactly what's been going on. We want Roger Bassington-ffrench for murder.'

'And we'll get him,' said Frankie, feeling better. 'How's Moira?'

'Feeling very bad. She's gone up to London – to a nursing home. She says she'll feel safe there. Now, Frankie, the start of the whole thing must be John Savage's death and his will. And it's quite likely that it's a forgery – that seems to be Bassington-ffrench's speciality.'

'I made notes after looking at the will at *Somerset House*,' said Frankie. 'The witnesses who'd signed it were Rose Chudleigh, cook – and Albert Mere, gardener. Then there are the lawyers who wrote it – Elford and Leigh, whose offices are here.'

'Right, I think you'd better visit the lawyers, Frankie. I'll go and see Rose Chudleigh and Albert Mere.'

* * *

They met again at lunch.

'Well?' asked Bobby.

Frankie shook her head. 'Mr Elford is lovely, but he was horrified at even the suggestion of forgery. He said Mr Savage insisted on the will being written in front of him and then Mr Elford watched him sign it and the servants signed their names to say they had witnessed it.'

'That says it's not forgery,' agreed Bobby. 'And Albert Mere is dead. Of Natural Causes – he was seventy-two. Rose Chudleigh left the Templetons and went to the north of England, but then she came back and married a man down here. Unfortunately she's a really stupid woman. Perhaps you could do something with her?

Rose Chudleigh, now Mrs Pratt, lived in a small cottage which was full of ornaments.

'We were interested to hear that you were with Mrs Templeton for some time,' explained Frankie.

'I wouldn't say that, Miss. Only two months.'

'Oh! I thought you'd been with her longer.'

'That was Gladys, Miss. The maid. She was there six months. I was the cook.'

'You were there when Mr Savage died, weren't you?'

'Oh, yes, Miss.'

'And you had to witness his will, didn't you?'

Mrs Pratt didn't understand.

'You saw him sign a paper and you signed it, too.'

A look of something like intelligence passed across Mrs Pratt's face. 'Yes, Miss. Me and Albert. I'd never done such a thing before.'

'Who called you to sign your name?' asked Frankie.

'The mistress. She came into the kitchen and asked if I would go outside and call Albert and would we both come up to the best bedroom. We did, and there was the gentleman sitting up in bed – he'd come back from London and gone straight to bed – and a very ill-looking gentleman he was. I hadn't seen him before. But he looked terrible. I signed my name and I went down to Gladys and said I'd never seen a gentleman look so like death, and Gladys said he'd looked all right the night before.'

And Mr Savage – the gentleman – died – when?'

'Next morning, Miss. When Gladys went in to take him his tea he was all stiff and dead. And then about two months later Mrs Templeton told me she was going abroad to live. But she got me a very good job up north and she gave me a nice present. A very nice lady, Mrs Templeton!'

Frankie rose. 'Well,' she said. 'It's been very good to hear all this.' She took a five-pound note out of her purse. 'You must let me leave you a little present. I've taken up so much of your time.'

'Well, thank you kindly, Miss.'

Frankie went and Bobby followed her after a few minutes, looking thoughtful. 'Did anything about that conversation seem strange to you?' he asked.

'Only one thing,' Frankie replied. 'Why did Mrs Templeton send for the gardener to come and witness the will when the maid was in the house? Why didn't they ask the maid?'

'I stayed behind to ask Mrs Pratt for Gladys's name and address.' Bobby's voice sounded so strange that Frankie looked at him in surprise. 'She didn't have her address, but her name . . .'

'Well?'

'*The maid's name was Evans*!'

Chapter 29 Evans

Frankie stared at him in surprise.

Bobby's voice rose excitedly. 'You see, you've asked the same question that Carstairs asked. *Why didn't they ask the maid? Why didn't they ask Evans*? So Carstairs must have thought exactly the same thing. He was investigating, just as we are. Evans is a Welsh name – so Gladys was probably a Welsh girl. He was following her to Marchbolt. He didn't know that someone was following him.'

'Why *didn't* they ask Evans?' said Frankie. 'There must be a reason.' Suddenly she looked at her friend with excitement. 'Bobby, if you're staying in a house, you never see the cook because she is in the kitchen all the time. And she never sees you. But a maid serves you at dinner. They *couldn't* have Evans witnessing that will – *because Evans would have known that it wasn't Mr Savage who was making it.*'

'But Frankie, who was it then?'

'Bassington-ffrench, of course! It was Bassington-ffrench who went to that doctor and made all that fuss about having cancer. Then the lawyer was sent for – a stranger who doesn't know Mr Savage but who will be able to swear that he saw Mr Savage sign that will. And it's witnessed by two people, one of whom hadn't seen him before – and the other an old man who probably had never seen Savage either.'

'But where was the real Savage?'

'Oh! I suspect they drugged him and kept him in the attic while Bassington-ffrench pretended to be him. Then he was put back in his bed and given the sleeping drug – and Evans finds him dead in the morning.'

'Gosh, I believe you're right, Frankie. But can we prove it? We must find Evans.'

Frankie groaned. 'That's going to be difficult.'

'How about the post office?' suggested Bobby.

They were just passing it and they went inside. There was no one in the shop except the postmistress – a young woman. Frankie bought a book of stamps, spoke about the weather and then said, 'But I expect you always have better weather here than we do in my part of the world. I live in Wales – Marchbolt. You wouldn't believe the rain we have there.'

The young woman said that they had a good deal of rain themselves and it had rained nearly every day, in April.

Frankie said, 'There's someone in Marchbolt who comes from this part of the world. I wonder if you know her. Her name was Evans – Gladys Evans!

'Why, of course,' the young woman said. 'She was the maid at Tudor Cottage. But she went back to Wales and got married – Roberts is her name now.'

'That's right,' said Frankie. 'You can't give me her address, I suppose? I borrowed a raincoat from her and forgot to give it back. If I had her address, I'd post it to her.'

'Well now,' the other replied, 'I believe I can. I get a postcard from her now and again. She and her husband have got jobs in the same house. Wait a minute now.' She went away and returned with a piece of paper. 'Here you are,' she said.

Bobby and Frankie read it together. It was the last thing in the world they expected.

'Mrs Roberts,
The Vicarage,
Marchbolt,
Wales.'

Chapter 30 Sensation in the Orient Café

Outside the post office, Bobby and Frankie looked at each other and laughed.

'She's been working at my father's vicarage all the time!' said Bobby. 'Now I see why Bassington-ffrench was so amused! Come on, Marchbolt's the next place for us.'

'Wait a minute,' said Frankie. 'We must get Badger's business sorted out. After all, he did save my life.' She opened her bag and took out a handful of five-pound notes. 'Give these to him and tell him to pay the people he owes money to and that Father will buy the garage and put him in as manager.'

'All right,' said Bobby. 'I'll deal with Badger. You go and get the car.'

Five minutes later they were driving out of Chipping Somerton.

It was getting late when they stopped outside the vicarage gate. A slim figure was standing on the doorstep.

'Moira!' cried Frankie. 'What on earth are you doing here?'

'The same thing that has brought you, I expect.'

'You have found out who Evans is?' asked Bobby.

Moira nodded. 'Let's go somewhere and talk. There's something I must tell you – before we go into the house.'

'All right,' said Bobby, moving unwillingly away from the door. 'But why . . .'

Moira stamped her foot impatiently. 'You'll see when I tell you. Oh! Do come. There's not a minute to lose.'

They gave in. About half-way down the main street was the *Orient Café*. The three of them went in and sat down at a table in the corner. A tired waitress brought them coffee.

'Now then?' Bobby said.

'I hardly know where to begin,' said Moira. 'But in the train going to London, I went along the corridor and . . .'

She stopped. Her seat faced the door and she leant forward, staring outside. 'He must have followed me,' she said.

'Who?' said Frankie and Bobby together.

'Bassington-ffrench,' whispered Moira. 'He's outside. I saw him with a woman with red hair.'

'Mrs Cayman!' said Frankie. She and Bobby jumped and ran to the door. They looked up and down the street but neither Mrs Cayman nor Roger Bassington-ffrench were in sight.

Moira joined them. 'Has he gone?' she asked, her voice shaking. 'Oh! Do be careful. He's dangerous – horribly dangerous.'

'He can't do anything as long as we're all together,' said Bobby, leading the way back to the table. 'Go on with what you were telling us, Moira.'

He picked up his cup of coffee. Frankie, sitting down, lost her balance and fell against him and the coffee poured over the table. 'Sorry,' said Frankie. She reached across to the next table, which had glass bottles containing oil and vinegar on it. She emptied the contents of the vinegar bottle into Bobby's cup and began to pour the coffee from her cup into the now-empty bottle.

'Have you gone mad, Frankie?' asked Bobby. 'What the devil are you doing?'

'Taking a sample of this coffee for Dr Arbuthnot to analyse,' said Frankie. She turned to Moira. 'The whole thing came to me as we stood at the door just now! You put something in our cups when you sent us running to the door to look for Bassington-ffrench, *Mrs Nicholson or Templeton or whatever you like to call yourself*.'

'Templeton?' cried Bobby.

'Look at her face,' cried Frankie. 'If she denies that's who she is, then ask her to come to the vicarage and see if Mrs Roberts recognises her or not.'

Bobby did look. He saw that face, that lovely, delicate face changed completely by terrible anger. She took a pistol out of her handbag, but Bobby managed to push it upwards as she pulled the trigger and the bullet passed over Frankie's head and buried itself in the wall of the *Orient Café*.

With a wild scream the waitress ran out into the street. 'Help! Murder! Police!'

Chapter 31 Letter from South America

It was some weeks later. Frankie had just received a letter from one of the less well-known South American countries. Having read it, she passed it to Bobby.

Dear Frankie,

I congratulate you! You and your young naval friend have destroyed the plans of a lifetime.

Would you like to know all about it? My lady friend has told the police almost all my secrets, so telling you won't do me any harm now. Besides, I am starting life again. Roger Bassington-ffrench is now dead.

I've always been a bad boy. My father covered up for me. But he sent me to Canada where I met Moira and her gang. She was a successful criminal by the time she was fifteen. We decided to become a couple, but we needed money – lots of it – and I wanted Merroway Court.

To begin with, Moira married Nicholson, who was coming over to live in England, because the police were beginning to suspect her. She was working with her gang in the drug business. Without knowing it, Nicholson was very useful to her.

Moira made several trips back to Canada, saying she was going to 'see her family'. She travelled under various names. She was 'Mrs Templeton' when she met Savage. He was attracted by her – but not enough to leave her most of his money or even give her very much.

However, we made a plan. The man you know as Cayman pretended to be Moira's husband and Savage was persuaded to come down and stay at Tudor Cottage. Then after a time Moira – well, you know what she did. She got the money "Savage" had left her and said she was going off to live abroad – in reality, she went back to Staverley and the Grange.

In the meantime, I was trying to carry out my own plans. My brother Henry and young Tommy had to die so that I could inherit Merroway. I had bad luck over Tommy. A couple of accidents went wrong and he survived. In Henry's case, he had a lot of pain after he'd had an accident hunting. I got him some morphia. He took it and soon became an addict. The plan Moira and I made was that he would go to the Grange for treatment and there he would take an overdose of morphia. Moira, of course, would be the one who would give him the drug.

And then that fool Carstairs started his investigations. Savage had written to him, mentioning Mrs Templeton and had even enclosed a photograph of her. When Carstairs came to England and heard the news of Savage's suicide and will, the story didn't seem right to him. Savage was a hard-headed businessman and while he might have an affair with a pretty woman, Carstairs didn't believe he would leave a huge amount of money to her and the rest to charity. The charity touch was my idea. It sounded so respectable! He decided to investigate.

By chance, some friends brought him down to lunch and he saw a picture of Moira on the piano. He recognized her as the woman in the photograph Savage had sent him and a few days later he went to Chipping Somerton and started to ask questions.

He didn't find Rose Chudleigh, but he found out Evans' married name and went to Marchbolt. I followed him. A push in the mist sent him over the cliff. When I was waiting for the police to arrive, I removed anything that could identify him, then put the photograph of "Mrs Cayman" in his pocket.

All was going well. And then your friend Bobby upset things. Carstairs had mentioned Evans to him – and Evans was actually in service at the Vicarage.

We were frightened we were going to be caught. Moira followed Bobby and put some morphia into his beer when he was asleep. But the young devil survived. You can imagine the shock that Moira got when she was coming out to meet me secretly one evening and came face to face with Bobby! She was so scared she nearly fainted. Then she realised that it wasn't her he suspected and she went along with what he was saying and made some more stories up. But the truth was that you and Bobby were a great danger to us.

Henry didn't commit suicide, of course. I killed him! When I was talking to you in the garden, I realised that you were too near the truth and that Henry had to die at once. I went straight in to deal with him. The plane that came over gave me the cover I needed. I shot him! The noise of the plane hid the sound. Then I wrote 'his' suicide letter, wiped my fingerprints from the gun and put the key of the study in Henry's pocket. I went out, locking the door from the outside with the dining-room key, which fits both locks. Oh, and I'd placed a firework in the fireplace which I timed to go off four minutes later.

Everything went beautifully. You and I were in the garden together and heard the 'shot'. A perfect suicide! And poor old Nicholson, who'd come back for a walking stick or something, was the perfect suspect!

Moira went off to the cottage. We believed that Nicholson's explanation of his wife's absence would be sure to make you suspicious. And where Moira really showed her quick thinking was at the cottage. She realized from the noises from the attic that you'd got me. She quickly injected morphia into herself and lay down on the bed, where you found her. After you all went down to telephone the police, she came up and cut me free. Then she went back to bed and the morphia took effect. By the time the doctor arrived she was genuinely asleep.

She was afraid you'd find Evans and so she hurried down to Marchbolt to get rid of her – and met you just as she was about to go into the vicarage! Then her one idea was to get you both out of the way – and made the greatest mistake of her life by trying to poison you. And then at the trial she told them all about my part in the whole thing!

So here I am starting life again . . . And all because of you and Bobby Jones. But I've no doubt I will be successful!

Goodbye, my dear,

Your affectionate enemy,
Roger Bassington-ffrench.

Chapter 32 News from the Vicarage

Bobby handed back the letter. 'Everything seems to have ended very well. Badger's being successful at the garage – thanks to your father, and also thanks to your father, I've got a marvellous job.'

'Is it a marvellous job?' Frankie asked.

'Managing a coffee estate out in Kenya? It's just the sort of thing I used to dream about.' He paused. Then he said, 'People come out to Kenya on trips . . .'

'Quite a lot of people *live* out there,' said Frankie.

'Oh! Frankie, you wouldn't?' He went red. 'Would you?'

'I would,' said Frankie. 'I mean, I will.'

'I've been keen on you always,' said Bobby. 'I used to be miserable – believing that though you liked me, you would never marry me because your father's an Earl and mine's just a vicar.'

'I suppose that's what made you so rude that day on the golf course?'

'Yes. It all seemed hopeless.'

'Hmm,' said Frankie. 'What about Moira?'

Bobby looked uncomfortable. 'Her face had an effect on me,' he admitted. 'And then, when we were tied up in that cottage and you were so brave about things – well, Moira just faded out. It was *you* – only you. So wonderful, so brave.'

'I wasn't feeling brave inside,' said Frankie. 'But I wanted you to admire me.'

'I did, darling. I do. I always have. I always will. Are you sure you won't hate it out in Kenya?'

'I will adore it!'

'Frankie!'

'Bobby!'

'If you will come in here,' said the vicar, opening the door of the sitting-room to bring in the members of the church who were meeting to discuss when they would next give away clothes to the poor.

He shut the door immediately.

'My son Bobby. He is – er – engaged to be married. A good boy, Bobby' said the vicar. 'At one time he didn't take life seriously enough. But he has improved very much lately. He is going out to manage a coffee estate in Kenya.'

One church member said to another in a whisper, 'Did you see? It was Lady Frances Derwent he was kissing!'

In an hour's time the news was all over Marchbolt.

Character list

Bobby Jones: the son of the vicar of the village of Marchbolt in Wales

Frankie (full name: Lady Frances Derwent): daughter of the Earl of Marchington and a great friend of Bobby's. She lives in both Marchbolt and London.

Badger Beadon: a close friend of Bobby's who lives in London

Roger Bassington-ffrench: the man who stays with the body

Mrs Sylvia Bassington-ffrench: sister-in-law of Roger, wife of Henry. She lives at Merroway Court, in the village of Staverley in Hampshire.

Henry Bassington-ffrench: brother of Roger

Dr Jasper Nicholson: a Canadian who runs a nursing home, The Grange, near Staverley, which treats drug addicts

Moira Nicholson: Dr Nicholson's wife

Tommy Bassington-ffrench: seven-year-old son of Sylvia and Henry

Alex Pritchard: the dead man

Mrs Amelia Cayman: the dead man's sister who identified him

Leo Cayman: Amelia's husband

Alan Carstairs: a Canadian explorer

John Savage: a wealthy friend of Alan Carstairs

Mrs Rose Templeton: who inherited most of John Savage's fortune

Mrs Rivington: a friend of Alan Carstairs

Mr Jones: Bobby's father, the vicar of Marchbolt

Dr Thomas: the Marchbolt doctor

The Earl of Marchington: Frankie's father, usually called Lord Marchington

George Arbuthnot: a young doctor, a friend of Frankie's

Mrs Roberts: the vicarage cook

Mr Frederick Spragge: lawyer to the Earl of Marchington's family

Rose Chudleigh, now Mrs Pratt: used to be the cook to Mrs Templeton

Gladys: used to be a maid to Mrs Templeton

Thomas Askew: landlord of the Angler's Arms where Bobby stays for a time

Mr Owen: an estate agent

Cultural notes

The British class system

At the time when *Why Didn't They Ask Evans?* was written in 1934, Britain had a distinct class system with rules that everybody knew and followed. The *upper classes*, the aristocracy, had titles, for example *Duke* or *Duchess, The Earl of Marchington* and were addressed as *my Lord* and *my Lady, your lordship, your ladyship*. In the story, Lady Frances (Frankie) is shown great respect by people due to her social position. She lives at Derwent Castle, and her family also have a large house in a wealthy part of London.

The middle classes were educated people who had to work for a living – they had professions in the law, medicine, education, business, and the Church (like Bobby's father, the vicar).

The working classes had limited education, leaving school at the age of 14. Many were employed in the houses of the wealthy. Bobby pretends to be Frankie's chauffeur, which would be considered a good job for a working-class man at the time.

It was not acceptable for the classes to mix socially and people were expected to have friends and marry someone belonging to the same social class. Although Bobby and Frankie were childhood friends, they no longer mixed in the same social circles when they grew up. Bobby feels socially inferior to her, and considers himself 'a nobody' in comparison to Frankie's friends. Although it had been acceptable for them to be friends when they were children, he feels he cannot have a close relationship with her as an adult.

Evans

The name *Evans* was a common surname in Wales, which is why Frankie thought there would be at least 700 Evanses in Marchbolt.

Private cars

Wealthy upper-class and aristocratic families often employed a chauffeur (see glossary). Frankie's family have a chauffeur-driven *Bentley* – a luxury car similar to the famous *Rolls Royce*. The second-hand car that Frankie buys for £10 would be the equivalent of about £450 today.

Inquests

In cases of sudden, violent or suspicious death, it is common to hold a public inquiry called an *inquest* to find out why the person died. The *coroner* is the person in charge of the inquest, and the official cause of death is decided by a *jury* – a group of twelve ordinary people from the local area.

At the inquest the coroner and the jury hear medical evidence, as well as evidence from any other people that may be relevant. The family of the person who died, and members of the public can also attend the inquest.

Once all the evidence has been heard, the jury gives its verdict – for example natural death, accidental death, suicide or murder.

The Church of England

Bobby's father is a vicar – the name for a priest in the Church of England. He is responsible for taking care of spiritual and religious needs of people in the local community. He leads church services – such as the six o'clock service on Sunday that Bobby is late for – and carries out ceremonies for births, marriages and funerals. Vicars are paid by the Church and live in a house called a *vicarage*.

Glossary

Key

n = noun

v = verb

phr v = phrasal verb

adj = adjective

adv = adverb

excl = exclamation

exp = expression

addict (n)
someone who takes harmful drugs and cannot stop taking them

addiction (n)
taking harmful drugs and being unable to stop taking them

alibi (n)
proof that you were somewhere else when a crime was committed

analyse (v)
to examine something using scientific methods in order to find out what is in it

anxiously (adv)
doing something in a worried way

aristocratic (adj)
having a high social rank

authoritatively (adv)
giving an impression of power and importance

Bentley (n)
an expensive, luxurious car

big-game (n)
large wild animals hunted for sport

bitch (n)
a rude name for a woman who behaves in a very unpleasant way

bitter (adj)
when a taste is sharp, not sweet, and often slightly unpleasant

bloodthirsty (adj)
enjoying violence and things connected to death

blurred (adj)
not clear

bounder (n)
a man who behaves in an unkind or deceitful way

breakdown (n)
a mental condition where you become so depressed that you cannot cope with your life

briskly (adv)
quickly and in an energetic way

bunker (n)
a large area on a golf course, filled with sand, that golfers must try to avoid

bush (n)
a plant which is like a very small tree

butler (n)
the most important male servant in a wealthy house

By Jove (exp)
an old-fashioned expression used to show surprise

chauffeur (n)
the person who drives the car of a rich or important person

cheque (n)
a printed form on which you write an amount of money and who it is to be paid to

chloroform (n)
a colourless liquid with a strong sweet smell, which makes you **unconscious**

Claridges (n)
an expensive hotel in London

cliff (n)
a high area of land with a very steep side, especially next to the sea

clue (n)
something that helps you find the answer to a mystery

coffee estate (n)
a large area of land where coffee is grown

coincidence (n)
when two or more events happen at the same time by chance

collapse (v)
to fall down suddenly because you are ill or tired

Colonel (n)
a senior army officer

concussion (n)
when you lose consciousness or feel sick or confused after you have hit your head

consciousness (n)
the state of being awake and not being **unconscious**

coroner (n)
the person who is responsible for investigating sudden or unusual deaths

cue (n)
a signal for an actor to begin speaking, playing, or doing something

cunning (adj)
able to achieve things in a clever way, often by deceiving other people

curtly (adv)
in a brief and rude way

damn (excl)
used to express anger or impatience

damned (adj)
used to emphasize what someone is saying, especially when they are angry

deceased (n)
a person who has recently died

discreet (adj)
being careful to avoid revealing private information

dose (n)
the amount of a medicine or a drug that should be taken at one time

drawing-room (n)
a room in a large house, where people relax or entertain guests

dyed (adj)
something that has had its colour changed

eagerly (adv)
looking or sounding as if you expect something interesting or enjoyable to happen

estate agent (n)
a person or company that sells houses and land

evidence (n)
information used in a court of law to try to prove something

fatal (adj)
an accident or illness that causes someone's death

fellow (n)
a man or boy

fingerprints (n)
marks made by a person's fingers which show the lines on the skin

forge (v)
to copy a banknote, a document, or a painting, to make it look real

frown (v)
to move your eyebrows together because you are annoyed, worried or thinking

funeral (n)
the ceremony that is held when someone has died

gaze (n)
the way a person looks at someone or something for a long time because they find them attractive or interesting

get hold of (phr v)
to find something

give evidence (v)
to say in court what you know about something

gloomy (adj)
unhappy and without hope

Gosh! (excl)
an exclamation that shows surprise

grain (n)
a tiny hard piece of something like sand or salt

Grange (n)
a large country house – in the story it is a **nursing home**

grin (v)
to smile widely

groan (n)
a long low sound of pain or unhappiness

guilty (adj)
having committed a crime or offence

habit (n)
something that you do often or regularly; an **addiction** to a drug such as heroin or cocaine

haughty (adj)
being proud and thinking that you are better than other people

heir/heiress (n)
someone who has the right to inherit a person's money, property, or **title** when that person dies

I say (exp)
an old-fashioned expression used to show mild surprise, interest or admiration

impersonate (v)
to pretend to be a person, either to deceive people or to make them laugh

influence (v)
to use your power to make people agree with you or do what you want

inject (v)
to put a liquid into someone's body using a needle called a **syringe**

innocent (adj)
if someone is innocent they did not commit the crime which they were accused of

inquest (n)
a meeting where evidence is heard about someone's death to find out why they died

inspector (n)
an officer in the British police

instinct (n)
a feeling that you have about something rather than knowing what it is

irritation (n)
a feeling of annoyance, especially when something is happening that you cannot easily stop or control

jaw (n)
the part of your face below your mouth and cheeks

jury (n)
the group of ordinary people in a court of law who listen to the facts about a crime and decide if the person accused is **guilty** or not

kidnap (v)
to take someone when they don't want to go and only give them back when you are given money

landlord (n)
the man who owns or runs a pub

lawyer (n)
a person who is qualified to advise people about the law and represent them in court

miracle (n)
something that is very surprising and unexpected

misadventure (n)
an unfortunate accident

M'lady (n)
used by a servant to address a woman who belongs to an aristocratic family

morphia (n)
an old-fashioned word for morphine, a very strong drug used for stopping pain

motive (n)
the reason for doing something

mud (n)
a sticky mixture of earth and water

Navy (n)
part of a country's military forces that fights at sea

nonsense (n)
something that you think is untrue or silly

nursing home (n)
a private hospital especially for old people

obsession (n)
an interest or worry in something which stops you from thinking about anything else

on the right track (exp)
doing something in a way that is likely to be successful

organ (n)
a large instrument like a piano that is used to play music in churches

out of character (adj)
unlike someone's usual behaviour or personality

pass away (v)
to die

peer (v)
to look at something very hard, usually because you can't see it well

pessimistic (adj)
thinking that bad things are going to happen

pile (n)
a mass of things that is high in the middle and has sloping sides

prospect (v)
to search an area to find gold, silver, diamonds etc.

prove (v)
to show that something is definitely true

pupil (n)
the small, round, black hole in the centre of the eye

reassuringly (adv)
making you feel less worried about something

ridiculous (adj)
foolish or silly

sacrifice (v)
to give up something that is valuable or important, usually to get something else for yourself or for other people

sanatorium (n)
a place that provides medical treatment and rest

sarcastically (adv)
saying the opposite of what is really meant

Savoy (n)
a very famous hotel in London

seduce (v)
to use your charm to persuade someone to have sex with you

service (n)
a religious ceremony that takes place in a church

sharply (adv)
doing something suddenly or angrily

shiver (v)
to shake slightly because you are cold or frightened

shudder (v)
to shake with fear or disgust

Siam (n)
a former name for Thailand

Sister (n)
a senior female nurse who supervises a hospital ward

sniff (v)
to breathe in air through your nose hard enough to make a sound

solid (adj)
something that is based on fact

stomach pump (n)
a machine with a tube that doctors use to get poisonous food or liquid from someone's stomach

suicide (n)
the act of deliberately killing yourself

superiority (n)
better than other things of the same kind

sympathies (n)
the feeling you have when you are sorry for someone who has had a bad experience

syringe (n)
a small tube with a thin hollow needle at the end

take the hint (exp)
to understand something that has been suggested in an indirect way

taunt (v)
to say unkind or insulting things

That's the spirit! (exp)
an expression used to show that you like someone's behaviour or attitude

title (n)
a word such as 'Lord' or 'Lady' that is used before someone's name to show their place in society

tip (v)
to give someone money to thank them for their services

torture (v)
to make someone suffer pain or anxiety

trace (v)
to look for someone or find information about them

track someone down (phr v)
to find someone after a long and difficult search

tragedy (n)
an extremely sad event or situation

trap (n)
a trick that is intended to catch or deceive someone

trial (n)
a formal meeting in a law court, at which a judge and **jury** listen to evidence and decide whether a person is **guilty** of a crime

the Tube (n)
the underground railway system in London

unconscious (adj)
in a state similar to sleep, as a result of a shock, accident, or injury

under someone's spell (exp)
to be influenced by, and do what someone wants you to do

Unsound Mind (exp)
a formal expression that means that someone is mentally ill

urgency (n)
something that is very important and needs to be dealt with immediately

verdict (n)
the decision that is given by the **jury** or judge at the end of a **trial**

vicar (n)
an Anglican priest who is in charge of a church and the area it is in

vicarage (n)
a house in which a **vicar** lives

victim (n)
someone who has been hurt or killed

well off (adj)
having a lot of money

will (n)
a document where you say what you want to happen to your money and property when you die

witness (n)
a person who saw an accident or crime

witness (v)
to write your name on a document that someone else has signed, to say that it really is their signature

wreckage (n)
what remains when, for example, a plane, car, or building has been destroyed

yard (n)
a unit of length equal to 36 inches or approximately 91.4 centimetres

your ladyship (exp)
used in Britain when you are addressing female members of the aristocracy

COLLINS ENGLISH READERS

The Agatha Christie Series

The Mysterious Affair at Styles
The Man in the Brown Suit
The Murder of Roger Ackroyd
The Murder at the Vicarage
Peril at End House
Why Didn't They Ask Evans?
Death in the Clouds
Appointment with Death
N or M?
The Moving Finger
Sparkling Cyanide
Crooked House
They Came to Baghdad
They Do It With Mirrors
A Pocket Full of Rye
After the Funeral
Destination Unknown
Hickory Dickory Dock
4.50 From Paddington
Cat Among the Pigeons